DATE DUE

JY 09 '08			
SE 2 4 08			
MR 3 0 '09			
AP 2 1 '09			
MY 2 6 '09			

Winter Wonders

**Center Point
Large Print**

**This Large Print Book carries the
Seal of Approval of N.A.V.H.**

Winter Wonders

Melody Carlson

CENTER POINT PUBLISHING
THORNDIKE, MAINE

This Center Point Large Print edition
is published in the year 2008 by arrangement with
GuidepostsBooks.

Copyright © 2004 by Guideposts.

The text of this Large Print edition is unabridged. In other
aspects, this book may vary from the original edition.
Printed in the United States of America.
Set in 16-point Times New Roman type.

ISBN: 978-1-60285-209-9

Library of Congress Cataloging-in-Publication Data

Carlson, Melody.
    Winter wonders / Melody Carlson.--Center Point large print ed.
        p. cm.
    Stories with a Christian perspective.
    ISBN 978-1-60285-209-9 (lib. bdg. : alk. paper)
    1. Bed and breakfast accommodations--Fiction. 2. Sisters--Fiction. 3. Large type books.
    4. Pennsylvania--Fiction. I. Title.

PS3553.A73257W48 2008
813'.54--dc22

2008005699

Acknowledgments

Once again, I want to thank Lorraine Martindale, Regina Hersey and Leo Grant, along with all the rest of the Guideposts Books and Inspirational Media Division folks. "Tales from Grace Chapel Inn" is really a group project, proving that it takes a village to raise a book. Thanks so much, everyone!

—Melody Carlson

Chapter ❄ One

Like a soft, downy comforter, winter had settled itself gently onto Acorn Hill. Alice Howard welcomed the slower pace of the quiet days and early evenings spent with a good book, the company of her sisters and a warm fire.

"I love January," she said to no one in particular as she laid another log on the crackling fire. "It's so calm and peaceful."

"Especially after the hustle and bustle of the holidays." Louise adjusted her glasses and started another row of knitting. She was working on an afghan in a soft shade of yellow.

"Oh, I don't know," said Jane as she refilled their teacups. "I've always found January to be rather dreary and tedious. Of course that might have been more true living in San Francisco than here. It always seemed the longest, grayest month to me. When I was in California I would sometimes gather up my seed catalogs and dream of summer and gardens, and I'd actually start counting off the days until spring would arrive."

"I used to feel that way too," admitted Alice, "but I suppose I've changed as I've grown older. I appreciate the quietness of winter more and more."

"As do I," said Louise. "Although my old bones do not always appreciate the cold weather."

Jane twisted a strand of her long dark hair and

smiled. "Well, give me a few more years and I'll probably be right there with both of you."

"Father loved wintertime," said Alice. "He said it gave him time to think. Sometimes he'd spend hours and hours just working on his Sunday sermon."

"Speaking of sermons," said Jane, "did I mention that Kenneth is taking a couple of weeks to visit his parents in Boston?"

"Oh dear, are they ailing?" asked Alice.

"No, but Kenneth is concerned that they're getting too old to keep up their house. His mother has been talking about moving into a retirement home, and he wants to help them check out some places."

"He is such a good son," said Louise.

"Who's going to preach on Sunday?" asked Alice as Wendell jumped up and made himself comfortable in her lap. She stroked the tabby's thick winter coat.

"Henry Ley is going to cover for him," said Jane. "Henry's been working with a series of audiotapes that are supposed to help him control his stuttering."

"Well, it is a good time for him to try preaching. There should not be too many people at church," said Louise. "Have you noticed how the congregation has thinned out since the holidays?"

"That's just because some of the snowbirds have gone to Florida," said Alice.

"Florida," Jane sighed. "Now, wouldn't that be lovely."

"*Yoo-hoo*," called a familiar voice from the kitchen, "anybody home?"

"We're in the living room, Aunt Ethel," called Alice.

"Oh, you girls look so snug and warm on this cold winter's night," said Ethel, unbuttoning her coat and removing her faux fur hat.

"Let me take those for you," offered Jane.

"What brings you out?" asked Louise as she set her knitting project aside and picked up a teacup.

"Pure boredom," said Ethel. She flopped down next to Alice on the sofa.

"Boredom?" echoed Louise. "You know what I always tell my music students when they complain about being bored. Only boring people get bored."

"Oh, *please*," said Ethel in a slightly offended tone. "I did not come over here to be lectured by my eldest niece."

Jane sat back down in the rocker and leaned forward with interest. "I think I know how you feel, Aunt Ethel. I was just telling these two that I never look forward to January. To be perfectly honest, I think it's a rather boring month too."

"It's not January so much . . ." Ethel eyed the plate of freshly made raisin scones on the coffee table.

"Help yourself," said Jane. "Tea?"

"Thank you." Ethel settled back into the sofa. "The reason I'm feeling bored has more to do with Lloyd Tynan than January."

Jane handed her aunt a cup of steaming orange pekoe tea. "What's up with Lloyd?"

"Lloyd has taken up bowling of all things."

"*Bowling?*" Louise's eyebrows rose as if Ethel had said that the mayor of their town had taken up skinny-dipping.

Ethel sadly shook her head. "He drives over to Potterston two nights a week."

"Two nights a week?" repeated Louise. "To bowl?"

"That's right. One night is for practicing and the other night is for the league."

"Lloyd is in a bowling league?" Jane giggled.

"That's right."

"Does he wear one of those shirts with his name embroidered on it?"

"It's baby blue, which is actually rather attractive with his eyes. He hasn't gotten his name on it yet, but I expect it's just a matter of time." Ethel looked as if she had bitten into a lemon.

Alice smiled. "I think it's nice that he's found a new hobby."

"But bowling?" She shook her head.

"It does seem a little odd," agreed Louise. "Lloyd does not seem to be the bowling type."

"And what exactly is the bowling type?" teased Jane. "Beer bellies, tattoos and bawdy jokes?"

"I don't know," said Ethel. "But, believe me, he seems to have really taken to the ridiculous sport. It's all Clark Barrett's fault."

"How's that?" asked Alice.

"One of the bowlers had to drop out of Clark's league for hip replacement surgery, so Clark invited Lloyd to join him one evening, 'just for fun,' he said.

And that," Ethel snapped her fingers, "was that. Lloyd was hooked. Apparently he knocked down all those silly things—whatever they're called—all at the same time."

"They are called 'pins,' said Jane, "and if he knocked them all down it was a strike. So does he wear the weird shoes and everything?"

"You better believe it. He even bought his own bowling ball. It's bright blue with a bag that matches." Ethel sighed. "I just never thought it would come to this."

"Come to what?" asked Louise.

"That he'd choose bowling over me."

"Oh, I'm sure that's not it," said Alice. "He probably just wanted to try something new. I remember Vera Humbert saying that she was on a bowling team in college. And she seemed to think it was lots of fun."

Ethel waved her hand. "Well, maybe it's fine for college kids. But at our age? Really."

"I think it's cute," said Jane.

"*Cute?*"

Jane nodded. "Yes. I can just imagine Lloyd in his new shoes and his baby blue bowling shirt sending the ball spinning down the lane."

"Good grief!" Ethel scowled.

"In fact, I think it might be fun to go and watch him sometime."

"You can't be serious, Jane," Ethel said.

Jane frowned. "That does sound pretty weird. I must

be more bored than I realized if I'm imagining that watching Lloyd bowl would be good entertainment."

Alice laughed. "Welcome to another Acorn Hill winter, Jane."

Jane looked somewhat perplexed now. "I don't remember feeling bored at all last year."

"That's because we were so busy getting the house fixed up," Alice reminded her.

Louise looked as though she was considering her boring-people speech again; fortunately she did not deliver it.

"Just think," said Alice, "now you have more time for your art and your jewelry and your cooking."

"That's true."

"Winter is a natural time to slow down and rest up," said Louise as she picked up her knitting again. "Even having no guests booked for the next couple of weeks is a blessing. I think this is God's way of giving us a much-needed break."

"I suppose." Jane sat back down, but still did not look convinced.

"So why not just enjoy this little reprieve, Jane," said Alice as she petted the happily purring cat. "Life will get busy enough in time."

"Maybe." Jane wore a funny little smile now. "If it doesn't, maybe I will take up bowling too."

"It must be catching," mused Ethel.

Chapter ❄ Two

The following day, when Alice returned home from her shift at the hospital, she was surprised to spot an unfamiliar car parked in front of the inn. It looked to be an old Thunderbird, maybe from the sixties. A warm shade of beige, the sporty but dignified car appeared to be in mint condition. She resisted the urge to peek inside to see if its interior was equally perfect. Instead she quickened her pace, hoping to discover who the mystery visitor might be. She knew that no guests had booked rooms, but perhaps this visitor was here about something else.

She came through the front door to see a tall, white-haired man, in a hat and an overcoat, looking around as if he was lost.

"May I help you?" she asked as she removed her jacket.

"Is this a rest home?" He said with a twinkle in his eye as he peered at her nurse's uniform.

She smiled. "No. It's a bed and breakfast. I work part-time as a nurse at the hospital in Potterston."

"Oh." He nodded. "Well, I was told that there was an inn beside the old church. I knocked on the door, and then just let myself in."

"And no one is here?" Alice glanced around. "I'm sorry."

"I was hoping to get a room," he continued. "Dusk overtook me as I was passing through your quaint little town, and I don't really see that well after dark. I thought I'd just stop for the night."

"We have plenty of room," she assured him as she stepped behind the counter.

"Hello?" called Louise.

"Out in the foyer," said Alice. "We have a guest."

"Oh my," said Louise as she came in from the kitchen. "I was not expecting anyone, and I just stepped out to run some errands in town. Is Jane around?"

"Apparently not." Alice smiled at the man. "I'm sorry. We must seem terribly disorganized. It's not usually like this. It's just that we weren't expecting any guests this week."

"Oh, I don't want to be any trouble," he said.

"You're no trouble," said Alice as she offered him her hand. "I'm Alice Howard, and this is my sister, Louise Smith."

"I'm Harold Branninger," he said and shook her hand.

"I can take it from here," said Louise, adjusting her glasses and picking up a pen. "Thank you, Alice."

"You're in good hands now," said Alice as she went upstairs.

"I can see that," said Harold.

Alice felt a mixture of disappointment and curiosity as she quickly showered and changed for dinner. She had been enjoying this little reprieve from guests, but now the man with the interesting car was going to change that. *Only for one night,* she reminded herself as she slipped into her comfortable loafers.

By the time Alice went downstairs, Jane had arrived home and was busy in the kitchen.

"I hear we have a guest," said Jane as she turned down the flame under a soup pot.

"His name is Harold," said Alice as she peeked in the pot to see what appeared to be New England clam chowder. "That smells delicious, Jane."

"I told Louise to invite him to join us for dinner," said Jane as she deftly slid two plump loaves of brown bread into the hot oven. "Since he's on his own and everything."

"That was good of you."

"Did you see his car?" asked Jane as she brushed off her hands on her white chef's apron.

Alice nodded. "Very nice."

"Yes, and in perfect condition. Did he say where he's from?"

"He didn't tell me. He did mention that he was just passing through."

"How old is he?" Jane asked this in a casual voice, but Alice could not help but wonder if her younger sister was interested.

Alice suppressed a smile. "Well, he's a tad older than you, Jane. I'm guessing late seventies."

"Oh." Jane nodded and then chuckled. "I was just curious, Alice."

Alice smiled now. "You have to feel a little sorry for any unattached male that shows up at a B and B run by three single women."

Jane laughed. "Oh sure, Alice, like we're all just

desperately looking for husbands these days." She shook her head. *"Not."*

Alice helped Jane set the table in the dining room, and before long the four of them were enjoying a supper of soup and bread.

"I feel like I landed in a fine feathered nest," said Harold after polishing off a second bowl of Jane's delicious chowder.

"I'm afraid that dinner wasn't very fancy tonight," said Jane.

He shook his head. "I've never been one for fancy foods. My late wife Lily always appreciated that I had fairly ordinary tastes." His face seemed to cloud over at the mention of his wife.

"How long has it been since you lost your wife?" asked Jane.

"Just a year now." He set down his spoon with a clink. "Sometimes it feels like a lifetime."

"What are you doing out on the road in the middle of winter?" asked Louise.

"I thought maybe a trip would help me to get past this . . . this . . . well, it's the anniversary of Lily's death this week. I thought that if I wasn't home . . . well, maybe it wouldn't be so hard."

"That makes perfect sense," said Alice as she began to clear the table.

"I should probably just sell my house and move to a condominium or something," he continued, "but it's hard to give up a lifetime of memories."

"Oh, just because you sell your house does not

mean you lose those memories," said Louise gently. "I sold my house last year, and I really have not regretted it at all."

"But you've got this lovely place," said Harold. "Didn't you say it was your family home while growing up?"

Louise smiled. "That is true. I suppose that makes a big difference."

"I'm sure you'll figure out what's best for you to do," said Alice. "I've heard it's good to wait about a year before making any big decisions after losing a loved one."

"Well, it'll be a year tomorrow." He sighed.

"Where will you be headed tomorrow?" asked Louise.

He shrugged. "Wherever the road leads."

Alice thought that sounded awfully sad and lonely. "You are welcome to stay on here."

He seemed to brighten. "Now that you mention it, I think that might be a good idea." He glanced at the three sisters and smiled. "If that's all right with everyone, I mean. I don't want to intrude."

Louise waved her hand. "That would not be the case. We are a bed and breakfast. This is what we do."

"And we'd love to have you stay longer," agreed Jane. "Believe me, it's been pretty quiet around this old house."

"I noticed you have a piano," said Harold. "Playing has been a lifelong hobby for me."

"Louise is the musician in the family," said Alice. "I'm sure she'd be happy to share her piano with you."

"Of course," said Louise with a warm smile. "It would be a relief to have someone else providing the musical entertainment. What do you like to play?"

"Well, I've never been big on longhair music." He winked at Jane. "And I'm not talking about the Beatles. I always went more for old show tunes. You know like from the Rogers and Hammerstein musicals. Lively songs that make you want to kick up your heels."

One of Louise's eyebrows rose. Alice suspected that Harold's musical taste might pose a problem for her more conservative sister.

"Show tunes?" Louise did not seem enthusiastic.

Jane laughed as she picked up the nearly empty soup tureen. "I would love to hear some old show tunes, Harold. I suggest we have our dessert in the parlor and see what Louise's piano is capable of."

Alice decided that Louise's piano was capable of some very lively sounds as she carried a tray laden with dishes of cherry cobbler into the parlor. Harold was playing "It Might As Well Be Spring" from *State Fair,* and Louise was sitting in an armchair with a pained expression on her face. If Alice did not know better she might have thought that her older sister was suffering from a toothache. Fortunately, Harold could not see Louise's face from where he was seated at the piano.

Jane was right behind Alice with the tea tray. They both waited until Harold finished playing the tune before they set down their trays and applauded with enthusiasm.

"Oh, look what Jane has made," said Louise, obviously hoping to distract Harold from playing any more, "cherry cobbler."

It was not long before dessert was gone and Harold was back at Louise's piano hammering out the theme song from *Oklahoma*. Only now, Jane was singing along with him. She was, as usual, a little off-key, but what she lacked in musical ability she made up for in enthusiasm.

"Jane, how on earth did you know all the words to that song?" asked Alice when they finally finished with a rip-roaring end.

"We sang it in chorus when I was in junior high," she told them, "back when they actually let me participate in music, instead of just lip-syncing. Our teacher, Mrs. Harper, had us do a lot of show tunes." She grinned at Harold. "This is fun."

"Well, that's probably enough for one evening," said Harold.

Louise looked relieved as she picked up her teacup. "Now, tell us, Harold. Where are you from and how did you manage to stumble across Acorn Hill?"

"Until I retired about thirty years ago, I was a pilot in the air force," began Harold. "As a result, we lived all over the world: Germany, Korea, Japan, Spain. You name it and I've probably been there. After I retired, we settled down in Philadelphia. That's where my wife was from."

"My late husband and I made our home in Philadelphia too," said Louise.

He smiled and tipped his head. "Nice to meet you, neighbor."

Louise smiled.

"I grew up in Altoona," said Harold.

Louise nodded. "Penn State country."

"That's right. That's my alma mater."

"My late husband went to Penn State," said Louise. "His studies were briefly interrupted by the war, but he finally graduated in '49."

"I graduated in '49."

"You might have actually known Eliot," said Jane in amazement.

"*Eliot Smith?*" said Harold.

"That's right," said Louise. "You knew him?"

"Knew him?" Harold slapped his thigh and laughed. "He was a good buddy of mine. We were fraternity brothers. The old Alpha Phi boys."

Louise shook her head in wonder. "That's amazing!"

Harold looked at Louise more carefully. "So, you're the one who finally snatched up ol' Eliot. He must've been quite a bit older than you, Louise."

Alice thought she actually saw Louise blush as she fingered her pearls with a thoughtful expression. "Eliot was fifteen years my senior. He was seventy-five when he passed on."

Harold frowned. "I'm so sorry to hear about that . . ."

"It was a relentless case of cancer." Louise cleared her throat. "It has been about five years now."

Harold nodded. "Well, I only knew him during our

college years, but he was a good man." Now Harold began playing the piano again, quietly, as if he was trying to remember something. "In fact, I still recall the time when Alpha Phi put on a show to raise money. Some of us seniors had just been to New York and had seen a new musical called *South Pacific* at the Majestic." He sighed. "Oh, what a time we had. Afterward, I purchased the sheet music for a couple of the songs and roped in some of the guys, including Eliot, to do a scene from the show. What a hoot that was. Eliot actually wore a grass skirt. You should've seen him." Harold was laughing hard now.

"No way!" cried Jane. "My brother-in-law Eliot in a grass skirt?"

"And coconuts!" Harold held his hands in the appropriate positions and laughed even harder.

Louise's blue eyes grew wide. "Indeed!"

"I'll bet I still have the photos somewhere," said Harold as he retrieved a handkerchief to wipe his eyes. "Oh my. Those were the days."

"It sounds like you had a lot of fun," said Alice.

"I can't get over the idea of Eliot in a grass skirt and coconuts," said Jane. "I'd love to see those photos, Harold."

"*Humph.*" Louise stood up now, placing her empty teacup back on the tray. "Well, I find it a little hard to believe. Eliot was a fine musician, and I never once heard him playing or singing show tunes or anything frivolous."

Harold winked at Louise. "Well, you know what

they say, Louise. Boys will be boys. And take it from me, Eliot liked to cut up now and then with the best of them. We all did. I realize you were still a little girl back then, but we were just fresh out of the service and a war that had been anything but frivolous. It was therapeutic for us to get a little silly sometimes." He smiled. "In fact, I still believe that."

"I think it's just what the doctor ordered," said Jane. "We all need to laugh more."

"It's certainly made me feel better," said Harold. Then he looked at his watch. "I must be keeping you ladies up. I will try not to wear out my welcome, and I will bid you good night. Thank you all for a most lovely evening."

"He's sweet," said Jane as soon as Harold was out of earshot.

"I think he's enjoying his visit," added Alice.

Louise shook her head. "Imagine that. Can you believe that he and Eliot were friends in college?"

"Why not?" asked Jane.

"Well, it is perfectly obvious that they were as different as night and day."

Jane poked her oldest sister. "I think Harold's taken quite a fancy to you, Louise."

"Well, that is just plain silly," said Louise as she gathered up her knitting. "Preposterous."

"I don't know," said Alice. "Jane may be right."

"Well," Louise just shook her head as she made her way to the door, "all I can say to that is *good night*."

Jane laughed. "Sleep well, Louie."

"Sweet dreams," called Alice.

"Do you think she'll dream about Harold?" asked Jane after Louise's footsteps could no longer be heard.

"Probably not." Alice balanced her tray of dishes as she flicked off the lamp by the piano.

"You're right. She'll probably have a nightmare about poor Eliot dressed up in a grass skirt and coconuts," said Jane with a giggle.

"Singing show tunes," added Alice.

"Poor Louise," said Jane. "Maybe I should take a mug of warm milk up to her."

Chapter ❄ Three

On her way to bed, Alice noticed a strip of light beneath Louise's door. She tapped lightly. "Louise?"

Louise opened the door. Her face was smeared with cold cream and her hair was partially rolled into sponge rollers. "Yes?"

"I'm sorry to bother you," said Alice. "I just wanted to make sure that Jane and I didn't hurt your feelings tonight."

"Sorry?" Louise frowned.

"Oh, we probably shouldn't have teased you about Harold. I guess we were just feeling a bit silly."

"Oh nonsense," said Louise, opening her door wider. "Come in here."

Alice stepped into Louise's room, pausing to admire the floral wallpaper. "This is really nice in here,

Louise," she said. "I think I appreciate these flowers even more in the wintertime."

"It is cheery." Louise pointed to the chair by the window. "Have a seat and tell me what is on your mind." Louise turned back to the mirror above her dresser and continued to roll her hair into the pink sponge rollers.

"You've started to roll your hair again?" asked Alice.

"Sometimes I just feel like doing it. Eliot always used to like how it looked after I had rolled it."

"Wasn't that strange about Harold knowing Eliot in college?"

Louise nodded. "It took me a bit by surprise, but then he is about Eliot's age, or rather the age Eliot would be now. Eliot would have turned eighty last fall. Goodness, that sounds old."

"It's not that far off, you know," said Alice as she ran her fingers over the green velvet chair. "Not when you consider how time seems to fly faster the older we get."

"That is true," Louise turned and looked at Alice, "but I do not always feel that old on the inside." She shook her head. "I have to admit, Alice, I did come up here tonight with my feathers slightly ruffled. With the talk of Eliot and Harold, and what you and Jane said, well, I suppose I was feeling a little like a schoolgirl. Then I looked in the mirror and saw this old silver-haired woman. It was so odd. I just stared and stared." She smiled sheepishly. "Then I got out the cold cream and the sponge rollers, as if I really thought I could keep the years at bay."

"You're a lovely looking woman for your age," insisted Alice, "and I do think that Harold was taking notice."

Louise waved her hand. "Well, just for the record, I am not interested in Harold Branninger."

Alice studied her sister for a moment. "Then why are you going to the effort? I mean with the cold cream and curlers?"

Louise sat down on the edge of her bed, her hands resting loosely in her lap. "I think it was the talk about Eliot in his college days." She reached over and picked up the silver-framed wedding photo from her bedside table and traced her finger over the image of Eliot. "He has been gone five years, but, goodness, I still miss him dearly."

Alice nodded.

"I still think of him as he was when we met—a distinguished-looking man in his late thirties. Oh, I was so smitten by him, Alice. Sometimes I still feel the thrill of it." She set down the photo and laughed. "Is that silly?"

Alice shook her head. "Not at all. I think it's sweet."

"For that reason, I firmly believe that Eliot Smith was, and will always remain, the only man for me. Does that make sense?"

"Perfect sense, Louise." Alice sighed. "Please, forgive Jane and me for teasing you about Harold tonight. I promise not to do that again."

Louise smiled. "Well, as long as I am being completely honest with you, and just between you and me, I will admit that I did find the old gentleman's attentions to be flattering."

Alice laughed. "Well, why not?"

"Although he is an atrocious pianist. I wanted to tell him to stop playing and singing before the neighborhood dogs started howling, but I managed to control myself."

"You did."

"But I am sure you will understand if I must excuse myself early tomorrow night. I mean, should Harold decide to entertain us again."

"I won't even question it."

"Thank you, Alice."

Alice said good night and tiptoed down the darkened hallway to her room. She was thankful that she had taken a moment to clear things up with her sister, and she would be sure to let Jane know that they must stop teasing Louise about Harold.

In her room, Alice picked up the letter she had received earlier that week from Mark Graves, her college beau with whom she had recently renewed acquaintance. Mark had posted a letter from Brazil where he was enjoying a stint on the Amazon. Traveling by boat with a biological research group, Mark was the veterinarian for the project, and he was having the time of his life. Even so, he had taken time out to write Alice once a week. She cherished his letters and kept them bundled up in a shoebox. Mark's stories were entertaining and interesting—even his hair-raising tale in the latest letter of how they had been invited to what turned out to be a horrible cock-fight. Naturally Mark and his fellow animal-loving researchers were completely outraged by the brutal scene. They were in a foreign country where cock-fights are legal, but before they slipped away into the night Mark and his colleagues managed to free several of the fighting cocks. Alice thought that was brave, if slightly foolhardy. But she understood and respected Mark's love for animals. Under the same circumstances, she might even have done the same. It was odd that he was working in places where animals were treated with such cruelty. She knew that it was hard on him to witness the brutality of events like bullfights and cockfights.

Alice put the letter in the box along with the others. She said her prayers before she went to bed and, as usual, she prayed for Mark's safety and good health as he continued his Amazon tour. She also prayed for their guest, Harold Branninger. She prayed that God would help Harold to get over the loss of his wife and be able to move on with his life.

"Help us to encourage Harold," she added. "Help him to find peace and comfort in our little inn. Amen."

Chapter ❄ Four

A lice was always glad when her part-time workweek ended and she could stay at home with her
sisters and be more involved with the comings and
goings at their bed and breakfast. She was always
equally glad when the weekend was past and it was
time to return to her job at the hospital. She liked the
sense of purpose and balance that this routine brought
to her life. As she went downstairs and smelled the
fragrance of Jane's vanilla Belgian waffles, she felt
thankful that it was her day off and that she could
enjoy a leisurely breakfast.

"Need some help?" she offered as she pushed open
the swinging door in time to spy Jane removing a
golden, crusty waffle from the iron.

"Morning," said Jane. "Sure, would you warm up
that maple syrup?"

Alice removed the metal lid and put the glass syrup
container into the microwave, watching it carefully
lest it get too hot. Then she set it on the kitchen table
and began to make a pot of tea.

"Any big plans for today?" asked Jane as she
poured more batter into the waffle iron.

"Not really. I thought I might go to town to see if
Viola's gotten in any new mysteries."

"Good luck," said Jane as she took a sip from her
large mug of coffee. "Last time I was in her shop, she
was on her high horse again about my reading 'trashy

novels.' Jane shook her head. "I was buying Oprah's latest book-club book, which is *not* trashy."

Alice laughed. "Viola just wants us to expand our minds. You should hear her taking me to task for reading mysteries."

"Makes you wonder how that woman stays in business."

"Supply and demand," said Alice. "She owns the only bookstore in town."

"Well, some of us know how to get our books online." Jane checked on the waffle but decided it was not ready.

"Our guest isn't up yet?"

"I think I heard him shuffling around a few minutes ago," said Jane.

"I, *uh,* I talked to Louise last night," began Alice, unsure how much to tell Jane. She decided on a condensed version, simply saying that Louise did not appreciate their teasing.

"She should lighten up a little," said Jane.

"Well . . ." Alice paused. "The reason it bothers her is that she really did love Eliot and she still misses him."

"Well, I don't want to make her feel bad." Jane checked the waffle again. "Maybe *I* should lighten up—on her."

Before long Louise and Harold came downstairs, and they were all seated in the dining room again.

"I haven't had waffles in years." Harold smacked his lips. "These look fantastic."

"*Yoo-hoo,*" called a female voice from the kitchen.

"That's Aunt Ethel," said Jane to Harold. "She lives next door and pops in now and then."

"We're in the dining room," called Alice.

"Oh, it smells divine in here," said Ethel, peering at the large platter of crisp, golden waffles. "I am completely out of coffee at my house," she continued, "and I wondered if I could beg a cup from my favorite nieces."

"Why don't you pull up a chair and join us," said Jane.

Ethel smiled. "Well, I must say these waffles look awfully tempting. Don't mind if I do."

Alice went to the kitchen to get another place setting. By the time she returned, introductions had been made. "Harold went to college with Eliot," said Jane.

"Our Eliot?" said Ethel.

Louise nodded.

"Well, isn't that something." Ethel smiled at Harold. "What brings you to Acorn Hill?"

"I needed to get away for a while," he told her.

"It's the one-year anniversary of his wife's death," said Jane. "He thought a road trip might help him to deal with it."

"That's right," said Harold. "As it turns out, I was right. Your lovely nieces here have proven good medicine for me."

"You should've heard him playing the piano last night," said Jane.

"I am surprised you did not," added Louise wryly.

Jane tossed a warning glance at her sister. "We had

the best time singing old show tunes. Harold knows them all."

"I love old show tunes," said Ethel. "I'm so sorry I missed that."

"We're going to do it again," said Jane. "At least I think we are. How about it, Harold? Are you up for another sing-along tonight?"

He shrugged and glanced at Louise. "Well, if everyone is—"

"Of course we are," said Jane. "Let's plan on seven-thirty. We'll have dessert in the parlor again. Aunt Ethel, you are invited too."

"Well, thank you," said Ethel.

"Why don't you bring Lloyd," suggested Alice. "I haven't seen him since the last church board meeting."

"*Humph.*" Ethel frowned. "You won't be seeing Lloyd Tynan tonight."

"Bowling night?" Jane asked.

"Our mayor has recently taken up a new hobby," Alice explained to Harold.

"No, it's not bowling night tonight," said Ethel. "Lloyd is heading for Philadelphia for a mayoral conference."

"Well, you can't fault him for that, Auntie," said Alice.

"It's not just that," said Ethel in a wounded voice. "He never seems to have time for me these days."

"He's just busy," said Alice.

"Too busy for me," said Ethel as she helped herself to another waffle.

"I find that hard to believe," said Harold.

Ethel stopped with her forked waffle in midair halfway between the platter and her plate. "Pardon?"

"I find it hard to believe that a man with any sense would be too busy for someone like you."

Ethel sat up a little straighter as she dropped the waffle onto her plate. "Well, thank you." She reached up and patted her red-tinted hair and smiled at the guest. "That's very kind of you."

Harold smiled. "When I left home yesterday, I never dreamed that I would find myself sitting here in the company of so many lovely women."

"Oh, do go on," said Jane with a teasing smile.

"No, I'm serious," said Harold. "Yesterday, I felt so down and blue that I wasn't even sure I could go on. So I packed my bag and just got in my car and started driving, hardly paying any attention to where I went. Then I ended up in this quaint little town named Acorn Hill and this lovely inn," he shook his head, "and I feel better than I've felt in ages."

Alice smiled. "Well, we're glad you came."

"That's right," agreed Jane. "And you're welcome to stay as long as you like."

"That is true," said Louise. "We do not have another room booked for almost two weeks."

Harold picked up his coffee cup. "Well, I may just take you up on that."

By the time Alice and Jane started clearing the table, Ethel had heard several of Harold's flying stories from the war.

"Goodness," said Ethel. "That was awfully brave of you."

He waved his hand. "It's what we had to do back then."

"So, do you have any plans today?" asked Jane as she refilled his coffee cup.

"I'm not sure what there is to do around here," he said. "I thought I'd get in my car and check out the local area."

"Is that your lovely car parked out front?" asked Ethel.

"That's my baby," said Harold.

"Oh, I just love T-birds," said Ethel with a coquettish smile.

"Well, I'll have to take you for a spin sometime."

"I'm heading out to Potterston," announced Louise as she stood up. "I have to pick up some new sheet music for my students. Does anyone need anything while I am out?"

"Potterston?" said Harold. "Is that nearby?"

"Yes," said Ethel and she proceeded to give him directions.

Alice went into the kitchen to help Jane clean up. "Looks like Harold's charming Aunt Ethel," said Jane as she wiped off the waffle iron.

"Oh, that just seems to be his way," said Alice as she rinsed the plates and loaded them in the dishwasher. "He's perfectly harmless, I'm sure."

"Well, Aunt Ethel is sure eating it up."

"Probably makes her feel better since Lloyd's a little distracted."

"Yes, maybe having Harold around will be good for Aunt Ethel."

"And he sure seems to be enjoying himself." Alice put the last plate in and closed the door just as the phone began to ring. "I'll get that," she told Jane.

"Hello, Cynthia," said Alice as she recognized her niece's voice. "Louise just stepped out, but—"

"That's okay," said Cynthia quickly. "I can talk to you about this."

"What I can I do for you?"

"I have a problem that I thought you ladies might be able to help me with."

"Sure," said Alice. "What is it?"

"Well, I'm the editor for a children's book being written by a woman, a kind of celebrity writer. That means she's not a writer at all, but has a big name that the publisher thinks would look great on the cover of a children's book."

"Oh, and that's a problem?"

"Yeah." Cynthia groaned. "I've been working with her for months, but getting absolutely nowhere. Now the book's deadline is only a week away, but we can't get any solid work done. She gets so distracted all the time by her other projects. I was wondering if I could bring her to Grace Chapel Inn for a week. So that we could work without interruption."

"Oh, that's a wonderful idea," said Alice. "We only have one guest right now, so we have plenty of room."

"Oh, I'm so glad, Aunt Alice. The publisher will cover the bill for everything—even the extra meals.

We would want to eat all our meals at the inn, if that's okay. Quite frankly I'd have been willing to sleep on the floor just to make this work out.

"Don't worry, providing the meals will be fine and you won't need to sleep on the floor, dear."

"I just knew that my family could help me."

"So, when do you plan to arrive, dear?"

"I'm going to see if she can leave tomorrow," said Cynthia. "Believe me, we don't have a moment to lose."

"Tomorrow's just fine. By the way, who is this woman?"

"Have you heard of Victoria Martin?"

"You mean Victoria Martin, the home and garden expert?"

"That's the one."

"Of course, dear, everyone's heard of Victoria Martin. That's who you're bringing here?"

Alice could see Jane mouthing the words now, with a look of horror on her face: *Victoria Martin's coming here?*

Alice nodded at her sister. "And when do you expect to arrive?"

"Maybe around dinnertime. Do you think Jane will mind?"

Alice made a funny face to Jane. "No, you know Jane never minds having extra guests for dinner."

Now Jane was furiously shaking her head and making a slashing signal across her throat.

"Thanks so much, Aunt Alice. I can't wait to see all of you again."

"We look forward to seeing you too, dear. And Victoria too."

Alice had barely hung up the phone before Jane exploded. "No way, she cannot bring Victoria Martin here, Alice. What on earth can she be thinking?"

"Hold on, Jane. Let me explain."

Jane was still firmly shaking her head. "Do you *know* who Victoria Martin is, Alice?"

"Of course. Everyone knows."

"She's the Domestic Diva, the Garden Goddess, the Queen of Design." Jane dramatically pulled on her hair. "She can't come *here*."

"Why not?"

"Look at this place," said Jane, indicating her kitchen.

"It looks great, Jane. I love the way you redecorated it last year and—"

"But to someone like Victoria Martin it'll look provincial and amateurish and—"

"You're making too much of this, Jane." Alice put her hand on her younger sister's shoulder. "Now, take a deep breath and tell yourself, Victoria Martin is just an ordinary woman like me. She puts on her trousers one leg at a time too." Alice giggled at the thought of Victoria Martin putting on trousers.

"You don't get it, Alice." Jane shook her head and sunk down into a chair. "This is my world. I mean cooking and gardening and decorating. It's something I take great pride and pleasure in doing."

"You're very good at it, Jane."

"Not compared to Victoria Martin."

"We should never compare ourselves—"

"How can I help it? That woman does it *all*. She has her TV shows and home care products and cookbooks and—"

"What difference does that make?" Alice felt confused now. Why should Jane care so much about someone like Victoria Martin?

Jane shook her head. "I don't know. I guess it's just really, really intimidating."

Alice sat down beside Jane. "I thought you'd love the idea. You have nothing to be intimidated by, Jane. You are a fantastic cook. Your garden is amazing. Your artistic talent at decorating is incredible. Why should you of all people be intimidated?"

Jane looked into Alice's eyes. "Really?"

Alice nodded. "I think Victoria Martin might actually learn a trick or two from you, Jane."

Now Jane laughed. "Be that as it may, I have a lot to do."

"And here's a little perk," said Alice. "Cynthia said the publisher will cover everything on the bill. Extra meals and whatever. I'm sure Louise will agree that it won't hurt our monthly finances at all."

"No, I suppose it won't. When did Cynthia say they were coming?"

"Tomorrow evening, in time for dinner."

Jane gasped. *"Oh my word!"*

Alice gently patted her on the back. "Now, remember just take deep breaths, relax, and tell yourself this is no big deal."

"Sure, I can tell myself that, Alice. It's just that I won't believe me."

Chapter ❄ Five

"Do you remember those old White Tornado commercials from the sixties?" asked Alice as she and Louise sipped hot cocoa out on the front porch. Fortunately for them, it was a relatively mild day, crisp and bright, with not a cloud in the sky.

Louise pulled her woolen scarf up around her neck and nodded. "I think so. It was for some house-cleaning product."

"Yes." Alice wrapped the red-and-black plaid blanket more snugly over her knees. "Well, that's what's going on inside our house right now."

"Is that why you met me out here?" asked Louise.

"Exactly. I had to take a break from it, and I wanted to tell you about Cynthia's plans before you went in."

"Well, it's a bit chilly, but the cocoa is a nice touch."

"Jane is into the spring cleaning a little early," said Alice.

"What's wrong with the poor girl?" asked Louise.

Alice laughed. "It's Victoria Martin."

"Victoria Martin? The author Cynthia is bringing here?" Louise frowned. "That name sounds familiar, but I'm not quite with you. Who are we talking about?"

"The Domestic Goddess of Home and Garden television." Alice made room for Wendell to jump into her lap, smoothing his coat as he settled himself into the warm woolen blanket.

Louise nodded. "Oh, yes. Now I remember. Wasn't she involved in some sort of copyright problem on one of her cookbooks?"

"Yes, but she was cleared."

"That's right, but, tell me, what does Victoria Martin have to do with Jane and the White Tornado?"

"Well, our baby sister is convinced that Victoria's visit is for a white-glove test, rather than to work with Cynthia on a children's book."

Louise smiled. "You know, Cynthia told me ages ago that she was working with some celebrity on a children's book."

"Apparently, it's still not written. The due date is next week, and Cynthia is getting nervous."

"I can imagine." Louise shook her head. "Poor Cynthia. She told me that her job could be hanging on the success of this silly book. Did she tell you the woman can't even write?"

"She mentioned something along that line."

"So Jane is in a dither because she thinks Victoria Martin will criticize our housekeeping, and Cynthia is in a dither because her job may be on the line. Good heavens. What is next?"

"Here comes Harold," said Alice, and she waved as the Thunderbird pulled up in front of the house.

"Oh, I almost forgot about our music man," said Louise. "I wonder what he has been up to today."

"Hello," called Alice as Harold came up the porch

steps. "Would you care for some hot cocoa?"

"That sounds delightful," said Harold as he joined them on the porch. "And is that real whipped cream?"

"Jane wouldn't settle for imitation," said Alice.

Harold sighed. "Ah, the country life."

"Well, we are not exactly country folks," said Louise, "but I suppose we seem a bit slow compared to Philadelphia."

"It's a pace I could get used to."

"So, what have you been doing with yourself today, Harold?" asked Alice. She was trying to think of a casual way to explain the frantic cleaning spree that was taking place behind the closed front door.

"I've had a marvelous day." Harold took a sip of cocoa and grinned. "I even turned out to be rather lucky."

"Lucky?" Louise frowned. "What do you mean?"

"At the track."

"The track?" repeated Alice. "What kind of track?"

"The racetrack," said Harold.

"*Racetrack?*" Louise looked surprised. "I had no idea we had horse racing around here."

"Not horses," said Harold. "Dogs. There's a dog track just outside of Potterston."

"Dogs?" Alice was puzzled.

"Greyhounds, to be specific. I picked a winner today."

"My goodness," said Louise.

Suddenly Alice remembered a story that Mark had told her during his last visit to Acorn Hill. "Isn't that cruel for the dogs?" she asked Harold.

"Oh no, the dogs love it. You should see them go."

"Chasing a mechanical rabbit?" queried Louise.

"That's right. But, of course, they never catch it."

"Is that really like fun, Harold?" Louise reached for one of the sugar cookies that Alice had brought out along with the cocoa.

"What do you consider to be fun, Louise?" asked Harold. "I'm curious."

"Fun?" She closed her eyes as if to consider this. "Fun is a classical concert in the park on a soft spring evening. Fun is seeing the children's eyes light up when they put on one of their little performances at church. Fun is a trip to the seashore on a warm summer day or hot cocoa on the porch on a sunny winter day." She sighed.

"Well, those things are nice," said Harold, "but they're not exactly what I would describe as *fun*."

Louise nodded. "I guess, like beauty, fun is in the eyes of the beholder. What is fun to me would probably be completely boring to you."

"And what's fun to me would probably be scandalous to you."

Her eyebrow lifted. "Scandalous? Please, tell us you're not involved in anything illegal or immoral or illicit."

"No, no, nothing quite that exciting. I do enjoy betting at the track now and then. And I used to play poker with my buddies every Saturday night, but most of them are long gone now." He sadly shook his head. "I may be old, ladies, but I'm not dead."

41

"Certainly not," said Louise.

"A friend of mine is a veterinarian," said Alice. "He told me a very sad story about a racing dog. A family adopted a greyhound that had been rescued—"

"Rescued?" repeated Louise. "What do you mean?"

"Well, Mark said that when the greyhounds get hurt, which often happens, or if they're past their prime, they are put down."

"Put down? As in killed?" asked Louise.

"Yes," Alice nodded solemnly, "and they're not always killed in a humane way. It's really awful."

"Oh, I don't think that could be true," said Harold. "Greyhound racing is a legal sport. The authorities wouldn't allow people to be cruel to dogs just for the sake of the sport."

"You wouldn't think so," said Alice, "but what if no one is paying any attention?"

"But why would they kill the dogs?" asked Harold. "They are beautiful animals, and the way they run is something to behold. Not only that, but they're very valuable. Now tell me, Alice, why would someone kill a valuable dog?"

"Probably because it is not valuable once it has been injured," offered Louise. "Why would they waste money feeding a dog that cannot run?"

"Exactly," said Alice. "Mark said that once the dogs can't race anymore, they are worthless to their owners. There are some places where people have set up greyhound adoption groups to save the dogs from being killed."

"I wonder if such a thing exists in Potterston?" ventured Louise.

"I don't know," said Alice, "but I'm sure it wouldn't be hard to find out."

Harold laughed. "I think you're creating a tempest in a teapot, ladies. I'm sure the dogs are well cared for. Really, you should come to the track with me and see for yourself. It was obvious that the owner of Copper King, the dog I bet on, loved the animal. I'll bet you that Copper is chowing down on a T-bone as we speak."

"But what happens when Copper can't run?" asked Alice.

Harold scratched his head. "I don't know the answer to that, but I'm betting that you're going to find out. When you do, you can let me know."

"And if I discover any inhumane treatment?"

"You prove to me that those dogs are mistreated, and I give you my word that I won't step onto a dog track again. But, if you ask me, those dogs were having the time of their lives down there. They are born and bred to run, Alice."

"That may be true. My worry is what happens to the animals when they can't run."

Alice's concern for racing dogs took her somewhat by surprise. She had not given these poor animals much thought before today, other than when she had heard Mark's story. She decided that she would look into the Potterston track first thing next week. In the meantime, there was work to be done in preparation

43

for the visit of Queen Victoria, Jane's name for their expected guest. It seemed that, at least in Jane's mind, this white-gloved perfectionist woman must surely rule.

Chapter ❆ Six

"Oh, do sing another one, Harold," insisted Ethel. "How about something from *The Sound of Music?* Do you know any of those songs? I just loved that movie. I still remember the night that my husband Bob and I went to the theater in Potterston to see it. It was the middle of summer and—"

"If you will excuse me," Louise stifled a yawn, "I think perhaps I will call it a night."

Harold winked at her. "My music scaring you off again?"

She forced a believable smile. "No, no, really, I am just tired. If I am going to be of any help to Jane tomorrow, I better turn in."

"In that case, I bid you *adieu.*" Harold began to play the good-bye song from *The Sound of Music.* "So long, farewell, *auf Wiedersehen,* good night," they all sang, waving to Louise as she made her exit.

Alice wished she could join her older sister, but she feared it might appear rude to have both of them leaving at once. She was more than a little worn out from all the cleaning that had gone on. She did not know if Jane would ever be satisfied. In fact, Jane had made a long list of tasks that had to be completed by the following afternoon. Alice noticed that Jane had even included "dust canning jars on back porch" on the list.

"Oh, Harold," gushed Ethel as they finished another song. "You are so talented. I don't know when I've ever had so much fun."

Jane was laughing too. "Yes, I'm so thankful that you're here, Harold. I think I needed this break tonight."

"Probably helps to get your mind off that silly Victoria Martin," said Ethel. "*Tsk-tsk.* I don't know why you're getting yourself all worked up about her in the first place, Jane."

"Because everything she does is so absolutely perfect," said Jane, as if that explained it.

"Oh, Jane," said Ethel. "She has dozens of staff people who do everything for her. She probably just sits around eating bonbons most of the time and telling everyone else what to do." She grinned. "*Hmmm,* actually, that doesn't sound like a bad life to me."

"You and Victoria will probably get along famously," said Jane dryly.

Ethel's eyes twinkled. "I'm sure we will. Just as long as she doesn't come over to *my* house. Good gracious, I'd die a thousand deaths if Victoria Martin looked into one of my closets."

"See!" Jane pointed at her aunt. "That's just what I'm talking about."

"Which room are you putting her in?" asked Ethel.

"Well, Louise thought I should put her in the Symphony Room."

"Of course," said Ethel. "That's her favorite, because she chose the decor."

"I was thinking the Garden Room might be more fitting since Victoria is as well known for her gardening as for anything else."

"I think the Garden Room is perfect," said Alice.

"I must say I'm enjoying my Sunset Room," said Harold.

"Thanks," said Jane. "I did that one and the Garden Room."

"It reminds me of a brief stint in Italy. So sunny and warm-looking."

Jane was beaming now. "That's what I was going for. Sort of southern France, or maybe even Tuscany."

"Well, you did a wonderful job with it." Harold smiled. "That's one of the things I really like about your inn. It's not fussy. I stayed in a few B and Bs with Lily. She loved those places, but I found them to be a bit uncomfortable with all their lace curtains and breakable objects and antique furniture everywhere."

"We wanted this to feel more comfortable," said Alice, "but it wasn't easy agreeing on things."

"It's plain to see that you three sisters really have a knack for it."

Alice hoped that Victoria Martin would see it that way, for Jane's sake. She hoped that Victoria would be kind and gracious. Jane seemed to be putting such stock in her visit.

"That's a great idea," said Jane suddenly. "Don't you think so, Alice?"

Alice blinked and looked at her sister. "I'm sorry, I must've been daydreaming."

"Aunt Ethel has just suggested that we host a sing-along night."

"Isn't that what this is?" asked Alice.

"No, something on a grander scale," said Ethel. "We could invite a few friends. I know that Lloyd would probably enjoy a musical night. If we can tear him away from his bowling ball, that is."

Jane laughed. "We can make it on a night when Lloyd's not bowling. How about a week from tomorrow, on Saturday? After Victoria Martin's departure. Is that okay with you, Harold?"

Harold nodded.

"We could dress up," said Ethel suddenly, "like characters from our favorite musical movies. Maybe I'll come as Eliza in *My Fair Lady*. I have a big purple hat a bit like the one that Audrey Hepburn wore."

"That's a great idea," said Jane. "Oh, this party will be just the thing to break up the winter doldrums for everyone."

"Doldrums?" repeated Harold. "I'd say that life here is anything but dull." Then he broke out into another song.

Alice slipped out of the room on the pretext of removing their empty dessert dishes, but what she really wanted was to get away from the music. She liked show tunes, but she had a bit of a headache—

probably from all the cleaning products that she had been using all day. She slipped on her jacket and went into the unheated sunroom. Even that place had made Jane's hit list. Everything in there had been vacuumed and dusted, and all the pillow coverings from the wicker furniture had been removed to be laundered. As a result, the room looked stark and bare. That would all change by the next day. Alice had overheard Jane on the phone with the local florist, Craig Tracy, ordering plants suitable for the cooler temperatures of the sunroom.

Alice sighed as she leaned back in the loveseat. She only hoped this did not turn out to be much ado about nothing. Just then Wendell hopped into her lap. He rubbed the side of his head against her hand in a way that she had always found comforting. She gave him a little scratch under his chin and wondered if he, too, was feeling displaced by all this busyness.

She looked out the window and up to the sky where a sliver of pale moon was just making its appearance. She knew it was selfish, but she resented all this hustle and bustle that had intruded onto her winter quiet. First Harold and his music. Now Victoria Martin. Yet she knew that people like Harold and Victoria had needs too. And perhaps their needs could best be met at a place like Grace Chapel Inn.

"Help me to be more gracious and generous," she prayed as she cuddled Wendell. "Help me to keep an open heart as well as an open home, and give me a good attitude as I help my sister Jane tomorrow. I

48

know that the best way to show Your love to anyone is by being a good servant. Please, show me how I can better serve those around me, putting their needs above my own. Amen."

Alice looked up at the dark sky again. It never ceased to amaze her at how refreshed she always felt after praying. She knew there was not anything special about her words or the way she prayed them. Perhaps it was just making contact, but then, of course, God was always nearby.

Chapter ❄ Seven

"Did anyone wash the front windows yet?" Jane asked Alice.

"Vera is working on it."

Jane pushed a damp strand of dark hair away from her eyes. "I know I'm a terrible slave driver," she admitted as she continued kneading a lump of dough. "I really appreciate you calling out the troops to help today."

"No problem," said Alice, sneaking a freshly made chocolate from a sheet of wax paper. "Everyone was excited to help out. There hasn't been a celebrity of this caliber in Acorn Hill since FDR's campaign stop in the thirties."

"And you can remember *that?*"

Alice grinned. "Very funny. I remember Mother and Father talking about it."

"Yoo-hoo," called Ethel. "Craig Tracy is here with more flowers."

"Tell him to bring them out to the back porch," said Jane.

"*Tsk-tsk.* Goodness knows why you need so many flowers." Ethel said. "Don't you think it's a bit extravagant?"

"Actually, Craig and I have an agreement. He happened to have more blooms than he needed this week, and I promised to repay him out of my garden next summer."

"Well, that was smart of you, Jane." Ethel patted her on the back. "I always did think you took after me."

Jane smiled patiently and then returned to her dough.

"Hey, Jane," called Craig from the laundry room, holding up a bunch of pale purple freesia and peach-colored roses. "Wha'd'ya think of these?"

Jane nodded. "Gorgeous."

Craig set the blooms in a galvanized bucket and came into the kitchen. "Smells good in here."

"Help yourself to . . ." Jane shrugged, "whatever. There are truffles there and some ginger biscotti by the stove and Alice just made a fresh pot of coffee."

"Sit down, Craig," said Alice, "and I'll get you a cup."

"This place is really hopping," said Craig as he picked out a chocolate.

"Thanks to Alice," said Jane, giving the dough a final whop. "She called out the troops."

"Well, they look like happy troopers," said Craig. "It seems we can always count on the ladies at the inn to bring some excitement to this little town."

"Really?" Jane did not look convinced.

"Seriously. This place used to be pretty dull before the inn got going. Seems like there's been something happening ever since."

Alice poured herself a cup of tea. "You don't miss the old quietness, Craig?"

He laughed. "Hardly."

"You young people," said Alice in a good-natured tone.

"It's good for business," said Craig as he snagged another truffle.

"Good for business?" Alice pulled up a stool across from him. "I thought Jane said you were doing some kind of swap on the flowers."

He grinned. "There's more than one kind of business."

"I told Craig that he could do all the floral arrangements and that we'd put his business card in a couple of conspicuous spots."

"*Ah*," said Alice, "and if Ms. Victoria is impressed, maybe she'll recommend Wild Things on the air?"

Jane nodded. "Who knows? Maybe she'll invite Craig to be on her show."

"Well, I seriously doubt that, but I still think this is kind of fun. I hope I get to meet the domestic diva before she skips town."

"Don't worry," said Jane. "We'll be needing some fresh flowers by the end of the week."

He gave her a thumb's up. "I'm your man, Jane."

"Did I hear that someone's looking for a plumber?" called a voice from the back porch.

"Come on in, Fred," called Alice. "The faucet in the bedroom that Victoria Martin will be using has just the tiniest drip."

"Can't have that," said Fred as he eyed Jane's truffles.

"Help yourself," said Jane.

"Why, thank you very much." He picked one up and popped it into his mouth. "*Mm-mm.* I figured it would be worth the trip."

"There will be more when you're finished," said Jane.

"Well, I'll get right on it then," said Fred. "According to Vera, this Victoria gal, whoever she is, might go flipping crazy over something like a dripping faucet."

"It's possible," said Craig. "I've heard stories."

"Oh, you guys," said Jane as she carefully laid a tea towel over her just-shaped loaves. "You make her sound like a monster. Good grief, she can't help it if she's a perfectionist."

"And you would know," teased Craig.

"I am not a perfectionist," claimed Jane.

Alice chuckled. "Well, what do you call a person who wants everything to be *just right?*"

"*Just right* is not necessarily perfection." Jane frowned. "Is it?"

"I plead the Fifth," said Craig. "I guess I had better get to work."

"Did you get the vases, Alice?"

"They're sparkling clean and right by the laundry sink," said Alice.

Jane picked up her list now, carefully checking things off. "Oh, Alice, I completely forgot something."

"What is it?"

"Could you run into town and get me some sheet spray?"

Alice frowned. "Sheet spray?"

"Yes. I told Sylvia about it last fall and she just started carrying it."

"What is sheet spray?"

"Well, that's not what it's really called, but it's a scented spray that you mist onto sheets to make them smell nice."

Alice nodded, although she really did not think it seemed terribly important.

"Get lavender," said Jane.

"Lavender," repeated Alice. "Sheet spray. Anything else?"

"Well, now that you mention it. I thought I was going to have time to go to the store for a few last-minute items, but looking at the clock now . . . oh, Alice, would you mind terribly?"

"Are you sure you want *me* to go, Jane? The last time I went shopping for you, I didn't do too well. Remember, I got the wrong kind of tomatoes and the wrong cheese."

"Give me a minute," said Jane, grabbing a pen. "I'll go over my list and be very, very specific so that there's no way you won't know what I mean."

"All right," agreed Alice. "I'm just not very experienced with all these gourmet foods."

Jane laughed. "These are hardly gourmet, Alice." She handed her the list. "Thanks, so much. I really appreciate it."

Actually, Alice welcomed the opportunity to get out of the house. It was feeling more and more like Grand Central Station. Her visions of a quiet weekend during a quiet month had completely vanished.

"Need a ride?" asked Harold when he and Alice nearly collided on the front porch.

"It looks like you're just coming in," said Alice as she hung Jane's big canvas shopping bag over her arm.

"Well, just momentarily," he told her. "I need a sweater under my overcoat. It's a bit nippy out here."

"Well, thanks anyway," said Alice, "but I think I will enjoy walking to town. I could use the fresh air and exercise."

He nodded. "Jane assured me that everything will settle down and get back to normal inside the inn by this evening."

"I hope you don't feel put out," said Alice. "Really, this isn't how things are usually around here."

"Oh, I know. Having this Victoria person coming to the inn is a pretty big deal."

"So, where are you off to today?" asked Alice.

Harold took on a sheepish look. "Oh, I thought, well, maybe I'd go see the races. I might poke around and check out the conditions you were worried about."

Alice nodded, though unconvinced. "So, you're not going to bet or anything?"

He grinned. "Well, now I wouldn't go that far, little lady. I guess I'll just have to sniff around and see how it goes." He brightened. "Hey, would you like to come with me? You could see for yourself."

She actually considered the offer but then shook her head. "Sorry, there's just too much to do at the inn today."

"I figured."

"But you can tell me what you discover. Maybe I can go some other time."

"Right." He tipped his hat, and Alice wished him a nice day.

It bothered her that Harold was going off to the dog track again. It was not that she had anything against people watching races and sporting events, but after their conversation, she had hoped that he might see dog racing differently. She promised herself that she would look into this more closely after the weekend. There was no sense in rushing to judgment about something one knows nothing about. Maybe Harold was right. Maybe those dogs did love to race. Maybe their owners did treat them with kindness and respect. Anyway, she decided as she entered the fabric store that she did not have time to deal with those issues anytime soon.

"Hello, Alice," said Sylvia. "How goes it at the inn?"

"It's buzzing like a beehive," said Alice.

"So how'd you escape?"

"I'm the errand girl today."

"*Aha.*" Sylvia grinned. "So, what can I do for you?"

"I need some sheet spray."

Sylvia frowned. "*Sheet spray?*"

Alice nodded. "It's used to make the bedding smell nice."

"Oh, you must be talking about our new linen potpourri spritzer."

"That sounds right. Jane said to get lavender."

Soon Sylvia had wrapped and bagged a glass jar of lavender spray. Alice was surprised at the cost, but figured a little bit must go a long way. "Thank you, Sylvia," she said.

"I'm hoping to at least catch a glimpse of her," said Sylvia.

It took Alice a moment to figure out what Sylvia meant. "Oh right. You mean Victoria Martin."

Sylvia nodded. "I'd love to have her visit my shop. She's an excellent seamstress, you know. I even sell her books here."

"I could mention that to Cynthia."

Sylvia winked at her. "Thanks, Alice."

Everyone seemed to want a piece of Victoria Martin. Alice began to feel sorry for the woman. What *would* it be like to have everyone grasping for your attention wherever you went? Would you ever get a moment's peace? How would you know whether someone was just being friendly, or if he was opportunistic? It could be confusing, not to mention demanding. Well, if Alice had thought that she had suffered a setback with this interruption of her quiet

January, she wondered how it would feel to step into Victoria Martin's shoes, as expensive as they must be, for just a day or two. Fortunately for Alice, that would never happen. Alice reminded herself to count her blessings as she started down Acorn Avenue toward the library, where she wanted to drop off a book. As she passed Time for Tea, she waved at its owner, Wilhelm Wood, who signaled her to come in.

"Hi, Wilhelm," said Alice, opening the door.

"Thanks for stopping, Alice. I have something for the inn." He smiled. "Do you have time?"

"Of course."

As Alice entered, classical music wafted toward her over the crowded shelves of ceramic teapots, fragile-looking cups, and boxes and boxes of teas.

She breathed in a deep breath. "Oh, Wilhelm, as usual, it smells so delightful in here."

"I recently created a new brew and I think it's magnificent," he told her as he led her to the counter in back of the shop. "It's a black tea with a secret mix of spices. Very warming and perfect for winter." He handed her a small brown package. "I'm calling it Wilhelm's Winter Spice."

"How much?" asked Alice as she extracted her wallet from her bag.

"Complimentary," said Wilhelm with a smile.

"Really?" Alice nodded. "How thoughtful."

"I, uh, I was hoping that Victoria Martin might get to sample it." He smiled. "Perhaps she might appreciate the fine blend of tea and spices and—"

"And want to know where in the world we got it?"

He folded his hands together and nodded. "One can only hope."

"Do you have a business card?" asked Alice, wondering if she had somehow turned into Acorn Hill's personal ambassador to Victoria Martin.

"I most certainly do." He handed her several. "Thank you, Alice."

"You're welcome. Thank you for the tea."

She dropped off her library book, then turned onto Berry Lane and walked toward the General Store. It was slow going because she was stopped by a number of friends and neighbors, all eager to hear more about the celebrity who was coming to town. It was not until Florence Simpson accosted her, however, that Alice felt herself getting irritated—and nervous for Cynthia's sake. She tried to explain to Florence that Victoria was coming to Acorn Hill for some *uninterrupted* quiet time in order to finish her children's book with Cynthia.

"It's not a social occasion," Alice assured Florence.

"Well, I should've known you would want to keep her to yourselves," said Florence in an offended tone.

"It's not that," said Alice. "It's just that Cynthia is facing a deadline and she needs to keep Victoria focused."

"That's not what I heard from your aunt. Ethel told me that there's going to be some big wingding at the inn."

Alice frowned. "A wingding?"

"Yes, and I heard that not only is Victoria Martin there, but also a renowned musician who has been performing nightly."

"Harold?" Alice shook her head. "I'm sorry, Florence, but Harold is just a nice gentleman who likes to play show tunes on the piano." Now Alice bit her lip. She knew that a sing-along night was in the works, but it was not up to her to invite people. If Jane and Ethel wanted to invite Florence Simpson, then that would be their decision. "Maybe you should ask Aunt Ethel to tell you more about Harold," said Alice, hoping that this might end the conversation.

"Don't worry," snapped Florence. "I intend to."

Alice controlled herself from rolling her eyes as she entered the store and headed for the produce section. Now if only she could manage to pick out some decent salad vegetables and make it to the checkout without further ado. No wonder Jane had asked Alice to come to town.

Chapter ❄ Eight

They should be here by now," said Louise for what must have been the fifth time.

"It's still early," said Alice as she glanced around the dining room. Everything looked perfect. At least it did to Alice. She was not so sure if Jane would agree. It was amazing how Jane could walk into a room, any room, and find something that needed tweaking. Whether it was a picture that was just slightly crooked, or a rose that had slipped just a millimeter, or a curtain not quite hanging straight, Jane would notice.

"Did you ask Cynthia when they would arrive?" asked Louise.

"Actually, I didn't. She said they'd be here in time for dinner."

"But she did not give a specific time? Like six o'clock? Or six-thirty?"

"Don't worry, Louise," called Jane from the kitchen. "I didn't fix anything that will be ruined—at least if they get here within the hour."

"Well, it is almost seven," said Louise. "And I have tried Cynthia's cell phone, but I keep getting her message service. I am worried."

"Maybe you should pray for her," suggested Alice. "That usually works better than worrying."

"Maybe I should." Louise said as she paced into the living room.

Alice looked around the dining room and wondered when she had ever seen it looking lovelier. The soft green walls seemed to glow in the candlelight of the pale lavender tapers. Jane had chosen pale lavender as an accent color in this room. Inspired by the freesias, Alice guessed. They would be using the fine china tonight, and Jane had talked Ethel into polishing the silver, even though Ethel was not invited for dinner on Victoria Martin's first night at the inn.

"I'm sorry, Aunt Ethel," Jane had said firmly, "but I think it's important that we keep this dinner small on her first evening with us. Don't worry, we'll make sure that you come over while she's here."

"Well," said Ethel in a stiff voice, as she polished a spoon, "if you think that's best."

"I do," said Jane. "Just for tonight, Auntie. Then we'll see how it goes."

Alice said another silent prayer for the safe travel of Cynthia and Victoria and before she reached "amen," the doorbell was ringing and she could hear Louise's voice greeting them in the foyer.

Although Alice had never considered herself the type to be starstruck, she suddenly began to feel very nervous. She looked down at her dark brown wool jumper, smoothing the front with her hands. Jane had said that no one had to dress up for the occasion, but Alice knew that she expected something beyond her usual weekend uniform of jeans and sweaters.

"Have they arrived?" asked Jane, suddenly emerging from the kitchen with her apron still on.

"Yes," said Alice.

"Does everything still look okay in here?" Jane glanced nervously around the dining room, pausing to adjust a folded linen napkin. "I think those candles still have a few hours left in them. Thank goodness, I got the dripless kind."

Alice patted her sister on the back and smiled. "Everything's perfect, Jane. Really. We should all just try to relax and enjoy this evening."

Jane nodded. "You're right, Alice. As usual, you are absolutely right." She turned. "I'll be in the kitchen if anyone needs me."

"You don't want to come out here and meet her?" Jane turned back and frowned. "Should I?"

"Of course. You're not just the cook, Jane."

"Should I take off my apron?"

Alice shrugged.

Jane hurried to remove her apron, gave it a toss into the kitchen and came out to join Alice.

"Here they are," said Louise as she led Victoria and Cynthia into the foyer. "My two sisters, Alice and Jane Howard. Co-owners with me of Grace Chapel Inn."

"It's a lovely place you have here," said Victoria as she handed Louise her fur-trimmed coat and Cynthia kissed her aunts.

"Do you need help with your bags?" asked Alice.

"They're in the trunk," said Cynthia with an expression that Alice could not decipher.

"Why don't Alice and I get them," offered Jane. "Louise can show you to your rooms."

Cynthia looked relieved as she handed over the keys. "Thanks, Aunt Jane."

"Cynthia looks a little frazzled," said Alice as they went out toward the sidewalk. "She must be worn out from work."

"Or from Victoria."

"She still has a whole week with her." Alice shook her head.

"Wow, is this Cynthia's car?" asked Jane when they spotted the silver Mercedes parked behind Harold's car.

"Maybe it's a rental or something," said Alice as she waited for Jane to open the trunk.

"My word!" exclaimed Jane when she saw the trunk stuffed with a very expensive set of Louis Vuitton luggage. "Is this *all* Victoria's?"

"Well, it doesn't look like Cynthia's."

Together they tugged and pulled until all the luggage, including one small dark suitcase, was out on the street. Then, taking two trips each, they hauled it up to the front porch. Fortunately, Cynthia met them there. "Need some help?" she offered.

"Thanks," said Jane. "You didn't tell us you guys were moving here for good."

"Yeah," said Cynthia. "That's what I thought too."

"Cool wheels," said Jane.

"The car belongs to my boss, and she threatened to fire me if I put a single scratch on it. She said she was only joking, but I'm not so sure. It was so nerve-racking to drive through traffic with Victoria's constant yammering about how she cannot afford to be taking time away from her businesses right now."

Alice patted her niece on the shoulder. "It's okay, Cynthia, you're with family now. We'll help you through this."

"That's right," said Jane as she opened the door. "This is what family is for."

"Everything looks great," said Cynthia. "Did you go to much trouble?"

"It was nothing," said Jane as she winked at Alice and they all made their way up the stairs.

"It's a little small." Victoria's voice was coming from the direction of the Garden Room, their best bedroom.

"I am sorry," said Louise. "It is the largest one in the house."

"Then I guess it'll have to do."

"Here are your bags," said Jane from the hallway.

"Put them right there," said Victoria, pointing to a space by the closet. "If they'll all fit." She shook her head. "I always overpack, but you never know what the weather might be, or what you might need to dress for. Samantha told me that Acorn Hill doesn't have much in the way of shopping."

"Samantha?" asked Louise.

"Isn't that your daughter's name?"

"You mean Cynthia." Louise frowned slightly.

"Cynthia, Samantha . . ." Victoria shrugged.

"Dinner is ready whenever you are," said Jane as she set the last bag on the chair by the closet.

"Yes, dinner," said Victoria. "I am starving. Saman . . . uh . . . Cynthia told me that the inn normally doesn't serve dinner, so I guess our meal will be simple."

"Oh, you will be pleasantly surprised," said Louise.

"That's right," added Alice. "Jane was a well-known chef in San Francisco."

"San Francisco?" Victoria's eyes lit up. "Oh, I just adore that town. Tell me, Jean, where was it that you cooked in the city by the bay?"

"It's Jane. Have you ever heard of the Blue Fish Grille?"

64

Victoria thought for a bit, then said. "No. I've never heard of it."

"Oh."

"Never mind," said Victoria. "I'm sure that whatever you threw together for us will be perfectly fine. And as I said, I'm famished. I haven't eaten since an early lunch. Just give me a few minutes to freshen up. I assume we're not dressing for dinner." Then she laughed.

"Whenever you're ready," said Jane as the three sisters exited what had once been their parents' bedroom.

" 'I assume we're not dressing for dinner,' Jane imitated Victoria as soon as they were halfway down the stairs.

"*Jane.*" Louise scowled.

"Well, really," said Jane.

"I know," said Louise, "but for Cynthia's sake, we must be polite."

"But, of course, dear sister," said Jane in a sweet voice. "I shall be nothing but polite—at least while Queen Victoria is within earshot."

"From the sound of things, I'm guessing your special guest has arrived?" Harold said as he emerged from the parlor where he had been holed up since six. Fortunately he had found a good book to read.

"She's here," said Alice.

"The *queen* will be down shortly," said Jane in a dramatic formal voice.

"Now, Jane." Louise shook her finger at her.

"Sorry." Jane made a face. "It's time for the kitchen help to get back to the scullery."

"May I help you?" offered Alice.

"That would be perfectly delightful," said Jane in her formal voice again. She offered Alice her arm, and the two glided toward the kitchen, noses in the air.

Alice tried to cheer up Jane as she filled the soup tureen.

"You've done a beautiful job with everything, Jane."

Jane rolled her eyes as she filled the breadbasket. "And all for *what?*"

"Because you love Cynthia."

Jane almost smiled. "Well . . ."

"And perhaps you wanted to impress Victoria Martin."

Jane sighed. "You're right."

"Some people don't want to be impressed."

Jane stopped her work on the salad plates, her hand in midair, holding a curly white strand of something Alice could not identify. Jane stared at Alice as if she had said something quite profound. "What do you mean?"

"There are some people who don't want to be impressed by *anyone.*"

"I've never considered that," said Jane, "but I think you're right. So, how did you get so smart, Alice?"

Alice smiled. "From experience. There's an administrator at the hospital who is always finding fault with everyone. Honestly, I think that even if she heard that one of the nurses brought someone back from the dead, she'd probably just shrug and act as if it were an everyday occurrence."

Jane laughed. "Maybe those kinds of people are afraid their importance will diminish if someone else is good at something."

"Exactly," said Alice as she set the soup ladle in the tureen. "I'm sure they must have a self-image problem. It's sad, really, because if they could only learn how to lift others up, they would probably feel a lot better about themselves too.

Jane shook her head. "Sometimes I think you're a genius, Alice."

Alice laughed. "I can assure you that I'm not."

"Well, you're awfully wise."

"It must be a God thing."

Jane put the last touch on the final salad, then went across the room and hugged her sister. "Oh, Alice, what would I do without you?"

"Serve dinner by yourself?"

"I can hear them coming into the dining room," said Jane. Then she put on a brave face as she picked up a tray of perfectly arranged salad plates and nodded toward the swinging door. "Okay, let's do this thing, Sis."

"I'm right behind you," said Alice as she balanced the steaming tureen and followed.

Chapter ❄ Nine

Jane had gone all out for dinner. Her menu included tomato bisque that was so creamy it seemed to caress the tongue, followed with salads that were not only true works of art but also delicious. Next was crown roast of pork with roasted pear and walnut dressing. Alice could not remember when she had seen such a meal before.

"I always put a dollop of crème fraîche on my tomato bisque," said Victoria.

"I used to do that too, but I've been trying to cut down on fats," said Jane. "If you'd like some . . ."

Victoria waved her hand. "No, no, don't trouble yourself."

Louise and Cynthia kept the conversation going during the salad course. Alice noticed that Victoria seemed to pick at her salad, but her plate was clean when it came time for the next course.

"The salad was divine," said Cynthia. "I'll have to remember how you did this so I can try it at home."

"It's quite simple," said Victoria. "I'm sure you'll have no problem."

Cynthia attempted to laugh. "Even 'simple' tests my culinary skills. Right, Aunt Jane?"

"You were getting pretty good in the kitchen last time you were here."

"Well, that's only because you were coaching me."

Victoria laughed loudly. "That reminds me of my

cooking show. Sometimes I get these people to come on, celebrity types, you know. And, of course, they've assured me that they are *experts* at some particular recipe. Well, the camera begins to roll, and it's not long before we can all see that they don't know the first thing about cooking. Oh, my goodness, it can turn into such a scene. And then at the end of the show I have to take a bite and actually act as if I like it." She laughed again. "I always keep a napkin handy, just in case."

Everyone laughed politely, and to Alice's relief, Harold began to question Victoria about her various projects. Thankfully, this kept the conversation moving smoothly until Jane brought out the entrée.

"Crown roast of pork," said Victoria with a look that was hard to read. "Well, I haven't had *this* for a while." She looked around the table now, as if she were searching for something. "Many people think they should serve Merlot with this dish, but I always prefer a nice light Pinot Noir, just barely chilled."

"I'm sorry, Victoria," said Jane, "but we generally don't serve wine at meals."

Victoria's eyebrows rose as if this were remarkable.

"Our father was the pastor of the church next door," Alice explained quickly. "He always felt that it was important not to set a bad example for his congregation."

"I see." Victoria took a sip of ice water.

"But I do agree with you," said Jane. "If I was serving this in the restaurant, I'd recommend a nice Pinot Noir."

"You would actually serve crown roast in your restaurant?" Victoria looked skeptical.

"Well, probably not, but if I did." Jane handed Victoria her plate with a stiff smile.

Alice was not sure what this conversation was really about, but she recognized that a sparring match was going on and she felt sorry for Jane. She wished that Victoria would say something nice. Perhaps it would have been better if the sisters did serve a bit of wine with dinner. In cases like this, it might actually be helpful—or not. Who could be sure? Alice said a silent prayer that dinner would move along smoothly without Jane's feathers getting too ruffled.

"Have you ever tried a bit of rosemary with this recipe?" Victoria pursed her lips together as if she had bitten into something slightly offensive.

"I like to use thyme and marjoram," said Jane, "but rosemary would be interesting too."

Victoria nodded. "Yes. It would probably be preferable to marjoram."

Jane did not say anything.

"I think it's wonderful," said Cynthia. "It melts in your mouth."

"It's delicious, Jane," offered Harold. "Don't know when I've had a meal half this good. Of course, my late wife Lily was never terribly comfortable in the kitchen."

"Now, I just don't understand that," said Victoria. "All it takes is a little practice, a good recipe book, and *anyone* can manage to cook. The problem is most people simply don't even try. I've often told my staff that I could probably teach a monkey to cook. Really, cooking is not that difficult."

"It is for me," said Alice. "I would never attempt to make a meal like this. When my father was alive I did all the cooking for us, but I always served very simple fare. Jane's the one who can really do miracles in the kitchen."

"That's right," said Louise. "Wait until you taste Jane's chocolate truffles. The town is just crazy about them."

"I created a special truffle," said Victoria. "It became so popular that we began selling it on my Web site."

"You can sell truffles on a Web site?" said Alice.

"Of course, you can sell anything on a Web site," said Victoria. "Have you ever looked at mine?"

Alice shook her head. "I'm not very computer savvy."

Victoria shook her finger at Alice. "Not good. There's no excuse for not using a computer these days. Back in the old days, when computers first came out and were so difficult to use, I could understand. Now all you do is turn them on and click the mouse. It couldn't be easier. And my Web site is simple enough to remember, it's my name. Someone tried to steal it early on in the game, thinking he could sell it back to me and make a lot of money. I finally had to have my attorney threaten to take him to court before I got it back."

At last it was time for dessert. Alice helped Jane clear the table. "Would you like me to put on the teakettle?" she offered.

"It's already hot," said Jane. "And the decaf is ready to go too. Just turn the pot on."

"You're so organized." Alice watched as Jane carefully placed raspberry chocolate tarts on dainty dishes and topped them with a small dollop of whipped cream, then added mint sprigs along with a few fresh raspberries.

"Where do you find fresh raspberries this time of year?" asked Alice.

"They grow them in hothouses," said Jane. "And they're not cheap. Don't tell, but I also used some frozen raspberries in the filling."

"I'm sure no one will notice," said Alice as she poured hot water into a fine china teapot.

"Don't be so sure."

Everyone seemed suitably impressed as Jane distributed the desserts. Well, almost everyone. It was hard to tell what Victoria was thinking. Alice thought she looked bored, or maybe just tired. Jane had told her that Victoria was about the same age as Alice but that she had probably undergone plastic surgery to make her look younger. There was, however, a certain look around her eyes that suggested she might actually be closer to Louise's age. Of course, Alice would not mention this to anyone.

"I grow raspberries at my home in New Hampshire. I just love eating them fresh, right off the vine.

They're so sweet and juicy in the summer." She picked up a raspberry with her fingers and shook her head. "These hothouse berries, well, they just don't quite cut it, do they, Jane?"

"I guess not," said Jane in a deflated voice.

"How many homes do you have?" asked Harold.

"How many homes?" echoed Victoria as if she had been asked a difficult math question. "Well, there's the one in New Hampshire. It's my main home, but I also have a home in North Carolina and one in Maui and another in Malibu and one in British Columbia." She paused as if to think. "And, oh yes, there's the villa in Tuscany."

"Tuscany?" said Harold, then he launched into one of his exciting World War II stories that managed to keep everyone amused and engaged until the last sips of coffee and tea were taken.

"That was a fantastic dinner, Aunt Jane," said Cynthia. "Let me help you clean up."

"That's all right, Cynthia," said Alice quickly. "I plan to help Jane. You've already had a long day of—"

"No, no." Cynthia tossed Alice a warning look. "I insist. You must let me help. I love being in Aunt Jane's kitchen."

Victoria glanced over at Jane. "Before my visit is over, you must let me see your kitchen, Jane. You know I am something of an expert in kitchen design. I expect I might be able to give you a tip or two."

"Oh, that's all right," said Jane. "I wouldn't expect you to—"

"It's no trouble, Jane. I would be glad to help."

Jane nodded as she began gathering up plates. "Well, thank you, Victoria."

"Don't even mention it." Victoria patted her lips with a napkin.

"Perhaps you'd like to join us in the parlor," offered Harold. "The ladies and I have been enjoying a bit of music in the evenings."

"Music?" Victoria looked somewhat interested. "What kind of music?"

"Actually," said Louise quickly, "you may have your choice. Harold likes to play show tunes," she cleared her throat, "and I play classical."

Victoria nodded. "Well, I'm in the mood for a bit of classical myself."

Alice released a sigh of relief as Louise, Harold and Victoria exited from the dining room. "I'm glad that's over," she whispered to Cynthia.

Cynthia nodded as she helped clear the last things from the table. "I feel so bad for Aunt Jane. I don't know what makes that woman so rude, but I've been putting up with it since this morning, and if you guys hadn't let me help out in the kitchen, I might've thrown myself down on the floor and kicked and screamed."

"Oh, that might be going to extremes, Cynthia." Alice smiled as she pushed open the swinging door. "In any case, we're always happy to get good kitchen help."

"You can say that again," said Jane as she ran water into the deep sink.

Cynthia went over and gently rubbed her aunt's back "I'm so sorry about Victoria, Aunt Jane. She can really be wicked sometimes."

"Is she *ever* nice?" asked Alice.

"Oh yes," said Cynthia. "She's nice whenever she's on camera, or when she's trying to sell something to some big-wig exec, or whenever she wants to get her way. Believe me, she can be very, very nice."

Alice shook her head and began transferring the leftovers from their formal dishes into storage containers.

"Are you crying, Aunt Jane?" asked Cynthia.

Alice turned around to look at her younger sister. "Jane?"

Jane wiped her eyes. "Yes, as a matter of fact, I am crying. I know it's stupid, but I can't help myself."

"Poor Jane," said Alice as she came over and patted her back.

"Your sympathy will only make it worse." Jane grabbed a tissue and swiped at her tears.

"Did she really get to you that much?" Cynthia looked very concerned now. "Maybe I made a mistake bringing her here. Oh, I'm sorry, Aunt Jane."

"No, no," said Jane. "It's not that, not completely anyway. I mean I might be just tired or maybe disappointed. I guess I'd just hoped that she'd appreciate *something. Anything!*" Jane sobbed even harder now. "It's—it's silly, I know. I feel like a baby carrying on like—like this. But I just want—wanted her to—to like me." Jane took more tissues and blew her nose.

"Oh, Aunt Jane," said Cynthia in a soothing voice. "I don't think Victoria likes *anyone*. Well, other than her pair of Dobermans. She seems to like them well enough. Their names are Rob and Roy. Believe me, it was all I could do to talk her into not bringing them with her this week. They're like her bodyguards, you know."

"Seriously?" Alice tried to imagine Victoria with a pair of big, aggressive dogs.

"Yes. She talks about them as if they're her children."

"Does she have children?" asked Alice.

"No, she's never been married."

"Oh."

"I'm sorry," said Jane as she began to recover. "I really didn't mean to fall apart like this. It's so unlike me."

"I know it is, dear," said Alice, "and I have just the remedy for you."

"What?"

Alice pointed toward the back staircase. "I want you to go up there and get ready while I draw you a hot bath. You will sit there and soak until you are ready for bed. Then you will get into bed and just read or whatever until you fall asleep."

"But, Alice." Jane waved her hands around the messy kitchen. "What about this?"

"You don't worry one bit about this," said Cynthia. "I will take care of it."

"I'll be back down to help you," Alice assured her,

"as soon as we get Jane taken care of."

"But—"

"No 'buts,' said Alice.

"That's right," agreed Cynthia. "And you're outnumbered so don't even think about arguing."

Jane held up her hands in mock surrender. "You win."

Alice followed Jane up the stairs, then went into Jane's bathroom and began filling the claw-foot tub with water. Next, she generously poured some lavender-scented bath oil into the flowing water. She found a couple of candles to light and turned Jane's radio on to a station that played the soft jazz that she knew Jane liked.

"There you go," said Alice as Jane stepped into the bathroom, now wrapped in her terry robe. "Enjoy."

Jane looked around and actually smiled. "You'd make a good lady-in-waiting."

Alice laughed. "Well thanks, I guess." Alice stepped toward the door and then paused. "Really, Jane, don't think about what happened tonight. As Cynthia said, that's just the kind of person Victoria is. It's no reflection on you. Honestly, I was impressed with your dinner tonight. You amaze me. I'll bet that Victoria couldn't possibly pull off something like that dinner without the help of all her dozens of assistants."

Jane dipped her hand into the tub to test the temperature and nodded. "You know, Alice, you might just be right."

Alice reached into her pocket. "I brought these up, just in case." She set two wrapped truffles on the shelf next to the tub.

Jane sighed. "When all else fails, go for the chocolate. Thanks, Alice."

Chapter ❄ Ten

"How's it going?" said Ethel as she sat down at the kitchen with a cup of coffee. She reminded Alice a little of Buffy, a small rusty-colored terrier that they had had as children. He used to sit on the kitchen floor as he waited eagerly for a doggy treat, tail wagging back and forth with anticipation. Alice could almost imagine Ethel's tail wagging as she waited for a tasty morsel.

"It's going okay," said Alice, looking toward Jane.

"Come on," urged Ethel. "A little more description, please."

"We had a lovely dinner last night. Jane made crown roast and—"

"I don't want to hear about the menu," said Ethel. "Tell me about *Victoria*. What's she really like?"

Jane turned around from the counter by the oven where she had been quietly stirring a bowl of some kind of yellow, lumpy batter. Alice had not asked Jane what she was concocting because she sensed that her younger sister, despite the bath and early bedtime, might still be feeling a little fragile.

"You'll have to get to know her for yourself," said

Jane. "Alice, could you get me a package of blueberries from the freezer?"

"Sure." Alice went for the blueberries.

"How do you suggest I do that?" asked Ethel.

"Why don't you join us for breakfast," offered Jane.

Alice set the blueberries next to Jane.

"Well, I haven't had breakfast yet," said Ethel. "I noticed the light on in your kitchen and decided to pop over to see if everything was all right."

Jane smiled. "I decided to get up early and get a head start on things." She glanced at Alice. "By the way, you and Cynthia did a great job on the kitchen last night."

"Thanks," said Alice. "We thought just in case Victoria comes looking . . ."

"Well, I'm not going to worry about that," said Jane. "I realized last night that it's foolish to try to appear perfect for Victoria or anyone else for that matter."

"Really?"

"Yes. It occurred to me that I should be more interested in pleasing God and myself than some snooty—" Jane stopped herself. "Sorry, I meant to control my tongue today."

"So she *is* snooty," declared Ethel in an I-knew-that tone of voice.

Jane shrugged. "You'll have to see for yourself. But, as I was saying, I decided that I need to focus more on pleasing God and myself. Everything I did yesterday was doing neither. So today I got up early, took a nice run and a long hot shower and came down here to putter around in my kitchen. And I decided to make blueberry muffins, with frozen blueberries, which I know won't measure up to some people's high standards, but they suit me just fine." She tossed the loosely frozen blueberries into the batter and gave it a stir.

"I love your blueberry muffins," said Alice.

"I do too," said Ethel, almost as if she were afraid to criticize her niece.

"So do I." Jane nodded. "And I am making *plain old* sausage and bacon and eggs to go with it. And if someone doesn't like it, well, she can just make her own breakfast or go see what's cooking at the Coffee Shop."

Alice giggled.

"I think your breakfast menu sounds perfectly fine, Jane. Besides, I've never known you to make 'just plain' anything."

Of course, Alice was right. Jane's breakfast *was* fit for a king, or even for someone who thought she was a queen. Alice sensed that Ethel was disappointed, because there was little small talk going on. Victoria was consumed with reading a small pile of e-mail that Cynthia had printed out for her, and Harold seemed intrigued by the newspaper.

"Well, we're off to work now," said Cynthia as she set down her empty coffee cup. "Unless you need help—"

"No," said Alice. "You two go work in the library. Remember that's what you came here for. May I bring you anything? Like coffee or tea?"

"I'd like some tea," said Victoria, "at around ten o'clock. And perhaps a little something to go with it?" She glanced at Jane.

"Of course," said Jane. "No problem."

"And I'd like a black tea," said Victoria. "If that's possible. I usually drink green tea in the afternoon, but I enjoy black tea up until lunchtime."

Jane nodded.

"Thank you." Victoria gathered her papers and stood.

"Have a good day, ladies," said Harold, pouring himself another cup of coffee.

"She doesn't seem like she's all that bad," said Ethel when she and the three sisters were back in the kitchen. "Oh, a bit presumptuous, I suppose, but she's not horrible. Did you notice that she looks much older in person than she does on television?"

"That's because they use makeup and lights to make you look good," said Jane as she set the remaining muffins in her covered pastry dish.

Ethel patted her hair. "I'd like to get my hands on some of that cosmetic help."

Louise chuckled. "So, how is it going with Lloyd? Did he make it back from the mayoral conference yet?"

"He was supposed to get back last night," said Ethel. "Although I haven't heard a word from him. *Humph*. He specifically mentioned that he wanted to be in church today to see how Pastor Ley handles things with Pastor Kenneth away."

"*Church!*" said Alice. "With all that's been going on

around here, I almost forgot that it was Sunday today. Not only that, but we forgot to invite Victoria to attend this morning's service."

Jane laughed. "Honestly, Alice, do you think she'd actually go?"

"Probably not. But we should at least invite her and make her feel welcome."

"They may just want to work all day," suggested Jane.

"Well," said Ethel. "They can at least take an hour off for the Lord's day."

"Not everyone sees it that way, Aunt," said Louise.

"I'll deliver their tea tray a little before ten so that I can remind them it's Sunday," said Alice. "And then I'll invite them to church."

"You're a braver woman than I," said Jane as she rinsed off a platter.

"Did you invite Harold to church?" asked Alice.

"I did," said Jane. "And he told me that he might come."

"Good for him," said Louise. "Now, I must excuse myself. I planned to practice at the organ, as well as warm up the sanctuary."

"Are you going to turn the furnace up?" asked Alice.

"Yes," said Louise. "It may only be one hour, but I am tired of freezing during the service. If anyone has a problem with it, I will just tell him that I will cover the additional expense."

"That's good of you," said Alice.

"No, it is mostly selfish," admitted Louise. "I can

hardly play the organ when my hands are so cold and stiff."

"Maybe you should get some of those fingerless gloves, Louie," teased Jane.

"Certainly," said Louise. "And perhaps a silk top hat to go with them as well?"

"Happy practicing," called Alice as Louise bundled into her warm coat.

Alice tapped on the closed door to the library at a quarter before ten. "Excuse me," she said as she opened the door.

"Is it ten already?" said Victoria as she removed her reading glasses.

Cynthia peered up from her laptop and looked relieved.

"It's a little before ten," admitted Alice, "but I wanted to let you know that you're both welcome to attend church with us this morning. I forgot to mention that at breakfast."

Victoria looked slightly surprised. "Church?"

"Yes, we always go to church," said Cynthia. "But if you'd rather work—"

"How long does it take?" asked Victoria.

"It's only about an hour," said Alice. "Our father always felt that a short service was more meaningful than one that dragged out for hours."

"Your father sounds like he was a sensible man." Victoria turned to Cynthia. "I suppose you'd like to go to church?"

Cynthia shrugged. "Well . . ."

"So, we shall go." Victoria looked down at her gray wool slacks and cashmere sweater set. "Does this mean we need to change our clothes?"

"No, not at all," said Alice. "You look perfectly fine. Lots of women wear slacks."

"What about my jeans?" asked Cynthia hopefully.

"I don't mind a bit," said Alice, "and I'm sure God doesn't either."

"What about my mother?"

"I guess that's between you two."

"Thanks for the tea, Alice," said Cynthia. "And tell Aunt Jane those scones look delicious."

"She just made them," said Alice. "They're still warm."

Victoria was already reaching for one.

"They're especially tasty," said Alice, hesitating to watch Victoria take a bite. In that moment, Alice saw Victoria's eyes flutter ever so slightly as if to say, "My these are good." Of course, her lips remained still.

Alice went out and closed the door behind her, before she hurried back to the kitchen to tell Jane.

"But she didn't say anything?" said Jane in a weary voice.

"She didn't say anything with her *mouth,* but if you had seen the look in her eyes." Alice tried to imitate it, which only made Jane laugh.

"Alice," Jane giggled. "You look like a love-struck teenager."

"Thanks," said Alice. "Speaking of teenagers, or almost teenagers, I need to get to church early to talk to some of my ANGELs about next Wednesday's meeting."

"See you there," called Jane.

Alice found several of her ANGELs and explained to them that they were going to do a baking project instead of what they had previously planned. "It's for the Mead family," Alice told the girls in a lowered voice. "Mrs. Mead will be getting home from surgery tomorrow, and I thought it would be nice to fix them a basket of baked goods."

"Sounds great to me," said Ashley. "Do we need to bring anything?"

"That's exactly why I wanted to tell you," said Alice as she handed the girls little slips of paper, each with one of the ingredients written on it. Alice had learned long ago that the girls became even more enthusiastic about helping others when they contributed something to the projects. She always took care not to ask for any expensive items from households that were struggling. Just the same, she allowed everyone to help.

"See you on Wednesday, Miss Howard," said Sissy.

"Hey, Miss Howard," said Jenny suddenly. "Why don't you ask Victoria Martin to come help us on Wednesday night? My mom says she always watches her on TV and that she's a really good cook."

"Yeah," agreed Sissy. "Maybe she could teach us how to make something really special."

Alice forced a smile to her lips. "Well, I'm not sure if she'll be able to do that or not, but I'll make sure that I mention it to her."

Alice went over to their regular pew and was surprised to see Ethel sitting there with Harold. Alice slipped in beside her and whispered, "Where's Lloyd?"

Ethel's eyebrows rose slightly. "I wouldn't have the vaguest."

"Oh."

Alice glanced over to where Louise was quietly playing on the organ to see that her sister was casting curious looks in their direction, as if to ask what Ethel was up to. Alice shrugged to indicate that *she* had not the vaguest. It reminded her of when they had been girls, sending secret messages back and forth, and she had to control herself from giggling as Pastor Ley made his way up to the platform.

Overall, the service went smoothly. Pastor Ley really did seem to be making improvement in his speech, although he did get stuck at one point, but then he took a big breath and smiled and just went on. The content of the sermon was uplifting, so Alice felt she was being completely honest when she said, "Pastor Ley, I believe that's the best sermon I've ever heard you deliver."

He grinned broadly as he shook her hand. "Thanks, Alice. Th—That means a lot coming from you."

His wife Patsy was beaming too. "Wasn't it wonderful!"

Alice nodded.

"I'm so glad, especially since we've got a couple of guests today," continued Patsy. Then, taking Alice's hand and stepping away from where Pastor Ley was greeting church members by the door, she lowered her voice. "Do you think you could possibly introduce me?" Patsy was looking at Victoria Martin now. Alice had noticed Victoria and Cynthia slipping into the church a few minutes late. They had quietly taken seats in the back but were now surrounded by several women in the congregation who were chattering away like magpies.

"I think we could manage that," said Alice. "If you can be patient."

Patsy nodded and stepped even farther away from her husband, who was now greeting Lloyd Tynan. "But, tell me, Alice, what is going on between Ethel and Lloyd these days?"

Alice glanced at Lloyd and noticed a slightly troubled expression creasing his usually smooth brow. "I'm not sure," she admitted.

"Well, Ethel certainly seems taken by your new guest."

"She does, doesn't she?" Alice watched as her aunt linked her arm into Harold's and they walked down the aisle toward the door. Ethel was gazing up into his face as if he had lit up the moon.

"Well, perhaps she's just trying to make him feel at home," offered Patsy.

"Perhaps," said Alice, but somehow she did not think so.

"Hello, Alice," said Lloyd as he made his way from Pastor Ley over to where she was standing. "Nice sermon today."

"It was, wasn't it?" She noticed Lloyd's glance moving in Ethel's direction. "How was your mayoral convention?"

"Oh, it wasn't really a convention. More of a conference," Lloyd hesitated, then asked, "Do you happen to know who the gentleman over there is?"

"Why, yes, he's staying at the inn. His name is Harold Branninger, and can you believe that he came upon our inn by accident, but he went to college with Louise's husband Eliot?"

"Really?" Lloyd peered at Harold with open curiosity. "That must make him fairly old? Eighty, you think?"

Alice shrugged. "I suppose. Although he looks younger."

"*Hmmm.*"

Alice felt sorry for Lloyd and hoped that Ethel was not carrying on like this on his account. "How's your bowling been going, Lloyd?" she asked to change the subject.

He turned and smiled. "It's been going pretty well. Who would've thought that old Lloyd Tynan would know how to throw a bowling ball?"

"Sounds like you're having fun."

"Oh, I am . . ." Then the sound of Ethel's overly loud laughter seemed to interrupt Lloyd's thoughts. He glanced to where the couple was now chatting with Pastor Ley.

"Harold was a World War Two pilot," Ethel said loudly. "Oh my, the stories this man can tell. We'll have to have you over to hear him play the piano sometime. He's just marvelous."

Lloyd seemed to bristle, then he adjusted his bowtie, nodded to Alice and made a quick exit. Alice watched the mayor going out the door. Was he hurt? Angry? Embarrassed? It was hard to know with Lloyd. Being the perennial diplomat, he was a master at keeping his feelings under control. She was ashamed of her aunt's behavior and planned to have a chat with her about it. In the meantime, she wanted to introduce Patsy to Victoria Martin.

Oh, to have life return to its quiet January normalcy, she thought as she went over to speak to Victoria. *Wouldn't that be grand?*

Chapter ❄ Eleven

Alice waited until the middle of the afternoon before she went over and tapped on Ethel's door.

"Alice!" said Ethel as if it were a surprise to see her niece at her door. "I was just making a pot of tea. Will you join me?"

Alice smiled. "Yes, that sounds nice."

Ethel peered out the door as she let Alice in. "It's been so overcast today, I wonder if it's going to snow."

"The weatherman hasn't predicted snow," said Alice as she removed her coat and scarf, "but it sure is cold out."

"Come sit by my fire and take the chill off."

Alice made herself comfortable in the rocker by the fireplace. She prayed silently for the right words to say to her aunt.

"Here you go, dear," said Ethel as she handed Alice a cup of tea. "It's a new blend."

"From Wilhelm?" asked Alice.

Her aunt nodded and sat down. "He said it's his secret recipe, Wilhelm's Winter Spice, I believe he calls it. I haven't tried it myself yet."

"Oh, this must be what he gave me to share with Victoria. I haven't tried it either, but I did brew a pot for Victoria and Cynthia before church this morning." Alice took a sip, and then nearly sputtered when she tasted it. "Oh!"

"Oh!" echoed her aunt. "Why would Craig get excited over this tea?"

Alice took a sniff of it. "It smells okay."

"But it tastes awful." Ethel made a face.

Alice took another careful sip, but it was so strong that she regretted giving the tea a second chance."

"I can't believe you actually gave it another try, dear." Ethel was standing up now. "Let's throw this stuff out and make a fresh pot."

A wave of apprehension swept over Alice as she followed her aunt into the little kitchen. "Oh dear."

"What's wrong?"

"I served that tea to Victoria and Cynthia."

Ethel chuckled. "Well, now Victoria will have something legitimate to complain about."

"Oh, how awful." Alice sat down at a kitchen stool

and watched as her aunt poured the dark brown brew down the sink.

"Did Victoria say anything about it?"

"No, I went straight to church afterward. Oh, poor Cynthia, she must think I'm nuts."

"Oh pish-posh. Just tell her it's Wilhelm's fault."

Alice picked up the brown packet of tea that was still on the counter. "I wonder what he put in here?"

"His *secret* recipe, of course."

Before long, Ethel had brewed a fresh pot of sweet-smelling Earl Grey, and they were seated comfortably by the fireplace again.

"So, what brings you to my little house?" asked Ethel as she put her feet up on the needlework foot-stool.

"I spoke to Lloyd at church today," she began, "and he seemed a little disturbed."

"Disturbed?"

"Seeing you on Harold's arm."

"Oh, *that*." Ethel waved her hand. "I was just having a little fun."

"A little fun?" Alice studied her aunt.

"Oh, why not?"

"Well, Lloyd seemed a bit troubled by it."

"Oh, I don't think he really cares one way or another," said Ethel a bit sadly.

"What makes you think that?"

"Well, he's so caught up in his own little world these days." Ethel sighed. "The truth is I fear that Lloyd has grown weary of me."

"Just because he took up bowling?"

Ethel looked truly sad. "But he never even invited me to go along."

"Would you go?"

"Probably not, but he could've at least asked."

Alice took a slow sip of tea as she considered this. "Aunt Ethel?"

"Yes?"

"Do you really care for Lloyd?"

"Of course."

"You two seem to have a fairly committed relationship." Alice sighed. "I was concerned when I talked to Lloyd. I thought you should know he looked unhappy."

"Oh, I'm not stupid, Alice. I *know* what you're saying." Ethel leaned forward now. "You don't approve of my flirting with Harold."

"Are you trying to make Lloyd jealous, Auntie?"

Ethel shrugged. "No, I know from experience that ploy doesn't work in real life, not the way it does in the movies. Although I was watching an old film the other night, and a little bit of jealousy did seem to solve all the heroine's problems."

Alice frowned. "But you really wouldn't resort to something like that, would you?"

"No, not on purpose anyway. I suppose I was simply enjoying Harold's attention. It's nice that someone around here appreciates me."

"Do you feel that Lloyd doesn't appreciate you anymore?"

Ethel set her cup down and stood up. She began pacing back and forth across her pastel-colored braided rug, rubbing her chin with each step. Then finally she stopped and turned to face Alice. "He seems to have forgotten all about me, Alice. He seems to like his old bowling ball more than he likes me."

"Oh, Auntie, I don't think that's true."

"We used to do *everything* together. Now I scarcely see him at all. The truth is I'm not like you and your sisters, Alice. You three seem to get along just fine on your own, but I'm all alone and I need a man in my life."

"But then why are you treating Lloyd like this, Aunt Ethel?"

Ethel frowned. "Like what?"

"Oh, you know what I mean. You said yourself that you were flirting with Harold after church today."

"I was simply introducing him to my friends," said Ethel.

"But you completely ignored poor Lloyd," said Alice. "How do you think that made him feel?"

Ethel sat back down and thought about what Alice had said.

"And what about poor Harold?" added Alice. "Is it fair to toy with his affections?"

Ethel waved her hand in a dismissive way. "Oh, that Harold, he's not taking me seriously for a single second."

"Maybe not, but still . . ."

"You do have me concerned about my dear Lloyd

now. I hope I haven't hurt him. Goodness, I wonder how I can make this up to him."

"I'm sure you'll think of something."

Ethel nodded. "I suppose there's no rush."

"*Aunt Ethel!*"

"Oh, don't worry, I won't use Harold to bother Lloyd anymore, but I might just wait a bit and see what Lloyd plans to do about this whole bowling thing."

Alice finished her tea and stood. "Thanks for the tea. I should probably get back and start helping Jane with dinner."

"Oh, certainly, she's not bending over backward to impress Queen Victoria again, is she?"

"No. I think she's planning a simple meal. Just the same, I should go help."

"Well, tell her that I said tea and toast should be sufficient. That woman could stand to take off a few pounds, if you ask me."

Ethel's comments about tea got Alice worried again. What had Wilhelm put in that tea anyway?

She decided to dash into town to his shop before she went home. She knew that Wilhelm's, unlike many of the local businesses, was open in the afternoon on Sundays. The bell tinkled merrily as she entered.

"Hello?" she called.

"Coming," said Wilhelm. He poked his head out of the backroom and using his hand to fan the air, he held up a wooden pipe. "Just enjoying a little smoke back here. Be right out, Alice."

He came out smiling.

"I didn't know that you smoked a pipe, Wilhelm."

"Oh, I try to keep it a secret. Mostly so Mother won't find out. She does not approve of tobacco of any kind. I have to hide my pipe and tobacco from her. You won't tell her, will you?"

Alice laughed. "Of course not."

"So, what brings you here today?" He rubbed his hands together. "Let me guess. I'll bet you'd like to get some more of my special blend tea."

"Well . . ." she cleared her throat, "that's what I wanted to talk to you about."

"What?" He frowned. "Is something wrong?" He slapped his hand over his mouth. "Don't tell me—did Victoria Martin hate it?"

"Well, I'm not really sure. You see, I served it to her this morning. Then I left and went to church."

He looked relieved. "Oh, then what's the problem?"

"Well . . . I hadn't tried your tea yet, but I was just at Aunt Ethel's, and she made us a pot."

He nodded expectantly, as if he was anticipating high praise. "And?"

"And, well, it wasn't very good."

If she had slapped him across the face, he could not have looked more surprised and crushed. "You didn't like it?"

She shook her head.

He scratched his slightly balding head. "How about Ethel? Did she like it?"

Alice shook her head again. "I hate being the bearer of bad news."

"I just don't understand it. Mother and I both think it's fantastic. We were almost through our first batch in a week. That's why I had her make the second batch just last Friday."

"Your mother made the second batch?" Wilhelm's mother was known in town as something of a scatter-brain. She tended shop for Wilhelm occasionally, but often when she did, something would go wrong.

"Do you think she messed up the recipe?" he asked.

"Have you had any of the tea from the new batch yourself?"

"No, she had it all packaged and ready for sale by the time I got back from my errands."

"And what my aunt purchased was from that batch?"

"It must have been."

"Do you have any left?"

"Of course." He held up a brown package. "It's right here." He opened up the package marked 'Wilhelm's Winter Spice' and took a whiff. "Oh no!"

Obviously, her nose had not been sensitive enough to detect the problem, but Wilhelm's was.

"Oh, this is terrible."

"I know. You should brew up a pot and taste it yourself."

"I don't have to," said Wilhelm. "I can tell it would be horrendous." He shook his head sadly. "Well, that explains it."

"Explains what?"

"Why my tobacco tin, the one that looks just like a

tea tin in order to camouflage it, was nearly empty today."

"Your mother put *tobacco* in your special tea?"

He took another sniff and made a face. "Apparently so."

"Oh, that's awful."

"I know. It was my favorite pipe tobacco too. Just the same it would be nasty in the tea." He peered into her eyes. "Oh, I'm so sorry, Alice. I cannot believe that I sent that over for—" he slapped his hand to his brow dramatically—"for *Victoria Martin!*"

"Oh, it could be worse, Wilhelm."

"I don't see how."

"Well, she didn't die from it."

"Good grief, do you think a person could die from ingesting tobacco?"

"Well, she didn't eat the leaves. Many men chew tobacco and," she made a face, "extract the juices. I suppose it couldn't be too harmful. Besides, I saw her in church and she was perfectly fine."

"*Victoria Martin went to church?*"

"She did."

He seemed to think this was as confusing as the tea catastrophe. "Oh my, maybe it was the tea."

Alice laughed. "I doubt it, but if that's the case maybe I should serve it to all our guests."

"Good heavens, no," said Wilhelm. "I hate to ask, but I'm sure I won't sleep a wink tonight if I don't." He took a deep breath. "Did you give her my card yet?"

Alice grimaced. "I, *uh,* I actually set it on the tea tray."

Wilhelm let out a low groan. "I am history."

She patted him on the shoulder. "Maybe she didn't see it, Wilhelm. They were busy working, you know. Maybe tea spilled on it."

He stood up straight and looked her in the eyes. "You must find out, Alice. I'll never be able to show my face in town again."

She smiled. Wilhelm could be so theatrical at times. "All right. I'll try to find out what happened."

"Will you call me, Alice?" He put his hands together as if he were pleading. "Please, as soon as you know?"

She nodded. "Yes. I'll get right back to you."

"Thank you." He picked up a package of tea that he knew Alice liked. "Here, you must take this for your troubles, Alice."

"Oh, you don't have—"

"I insist. I am so embarrassed. And, sometime, when we've recovered from this shock, you must try the real special blend." He shook his head. "It's really excellent, unlike—" he held the package of tobacco tea at arm's length as if it were poison—"this horrible stuff." Then he threw it into the trash.

Poor Wilhelm, thought Alice, as she hurried toward home. She felt a bit sorry for Cynthia and Victoria too. Had they actually drunk that foul-tasting brew?

Chapter ❄ Twelve

By the time Alice got home, Jane was already working on dinner. "Sorry, I'm so late," said Alice as she hung up her coat and reached for an apron.

"It's okay." Jane handed her some potatoes and a peeler.

"You won't believe what I just found out," she began and then told Jane the whole tea story until they were both laughing so hard they had tears coming down their faces.

"*Stop* it!" said Jane, holding her sides. "You keep this up, Alice, and I'm going to banish you from my kitchen."

"I'm sorry," Alice wiped her eyes, "but has Cynthia mentioned anything about the tea? Good grief, she probably thought we were trying to poison them."

"She never said a single word about it," said Jane. "Although, as I recall, she was having coffee. She brought the tea tray back in here this afternoon, and I made them some fresh green tea, along with a plate of ginger biscotti." Jane thought for a moment. "The teapot was nearly empty when I poured it into the sink and rinsed it out."

"*Nearly empty?*" Alice shook her head. "That can't be." Then she went over to the tea cupboard and took out the brown package of Wilhelm's Winter Spice. She opened it and held it out for her sister to sniff.

"Yuck!" Jane pulled her head back. "I can tell there's something wrong with that."

Alice nodded. "I'm afraid you're right. But why would they drink it?"

"Maybe Cynthia realized it was bad and poured it into the potted fern." Jane frowned. "Although, I hope not. That plant was just starting to look good."

It was not until dinner that the mystery of the tea was solved. After a bit of small talk about their work on the book, and Victoria's assessment of the service at Grace Chapel, or more specifically, the "preacher with the funny way of talking," Alice managed to bring up the tea.

"I wanted to say something about this morning's tea," she began, wondering just how a person said something like this.

"Oh yes," said Victoria suddenly. "I told Cynthia to remind me to say something about that."

Alice flushed. "I—"

"That was the *best* tea," said Victoria. "*Really.* I even kept the business card for the shop, which is something I almost never do. As you might imagine, I am handed cards every time I turn around. Anyway, I told Cynthia that we simply *must* pay this place a special visit. I'd like to buy several pounds of that tea if possible."

Alice was so shocked she was speechless. She hoped her mouth was not hanging open.

"*Uh,* it's a special blend," said Jane quickly. "Wilhelm Wood, the proprietor of Time for Tea, used a secret recipe. It's called Wilhelm's Winter Spice."

Louise's eyebrows lifted as she looked from Jane to Alice. They had shared the story with her just shortly before dinner.

"I told Victoria that we could visit Time for Tea tomorrow," said Cynthia innocently. "I think we should be due for a walk around the town by then."

"Oh yes," said Louise. "Victoria might enjoy our quaint little town."

"Now that I've sampled this special tea, I *am* interested," said Victoria. "I sometimes find items that I can carry on my Web site in little hole-in-the-wall places just like this."

Alice could not wait for dinner to end so she could call Wilhelm. She made sure that Victoria and Cynthia were well out of earshot, off listening to Harold playing show tunes, before she picked up the phone and called Wilhelm at home.

It took several repetitions before Wilhelm understood what she was telling him. Even then he sounded skeptical. Meanwhile, Jane and Louise were cleaning up the kitchen but were also listening, barely suppressing laughter and making it even more difficult for Alice to get her message across.

"I am not putting you on, Wilhelm. Victoria said she loves your special blend tea."

"The tea with the tobacco?"

"Yes. Wilhelm's Winter Spice, and it is *the tea with the tobacco.*"

"And this is *the* Victoria Martin, famed cuisine chef,

expert in all areas of house and garden and food and wine?"

"Yes. I know it sounds crazy, but that's what she said. I even have witnesses." Alice glanced at her sisters, who were now laughing aloud. "Well, they might not be the most reliable witnesses."

Jane grabbed the phone from Alice. "Listen, Wilhelm, this is Jane. What Alice is saying is true. Victoria thinks your stinky tobacco tea is the bee's knees. Not only that, but she plans to pay you a visit tomorrow." Jane rolled her eyes at whatever the poor man was saying on the other end.

"Calm down, Wilhelm," she told him. "Now, listen to me. Take a deep breath and just listen, okay?" She winked at Alice. "Do you have any more of that tobacco?" She paused. "Good, good. Now, your mother probably doesn't know exactly how she mixed it, but you might ask her." Another pause. "Yes, we still have our package of tea, and I'm guessing Aunt Ethel has hers, since she probably plans to return it for a full refund."

Louise and Alice listened as Jane and Wilhelm discussed the process of figuring out what went into that tea and being prepared to make more. "Of course, you do realize that you'll have to tell her about the secret ingredient . . . That's okay, Wilhelm, I know you do. But, hey, you know what they say you should do when life gives you lemons." She laughed and hung up, and then turned to her sisters. "In a very stiff voice, Wilhelm just informed me that my little adage couldn't possibly apply to tobacco and tea."

When the sisters had recovered, they took dessert and tea (a nice decaffeinated jasmine) into the parlor.

"Are you really up for Harold's music tonight?" Jane asked Louise before they entered the room.

"After hearing about the tobacco tea?" Louise grinned. "I think I am up for almost anything."

Harold was just winding down a song as the sisters came in.

"That sounded great," said Jane as she began pouring tea.

"Time for a break," said Harold as he pushed himself away from the piano. "And this looks worthy of breaking for."

"Oh, it's only crème caramel," said Jane.

The room got quiet as they all enjoyed their custards. Alice sneaked a peek at Victoria, who seemed happy to eat every last bit.

"You know," said Victoria as she picked up her teacup and leaned back into the easy chair. "Custard was one of the first things I learned to cook." She sighed as if enjoying a good memory. "It was my grandmother who taught me how to make it. Oh, it wasn't sophisticated like this. My grandmother didn't know a thing about French cuisine. Her recipe was a simple farm one. Steamed milk and farm-fresh eggs." She sighed again. "It always makes me happy just remembering."

Alice cleared her throat. "That reminds me of something, Victoria."

Victoria snapped back to attention, and Alice almost regretted interrupting her little reverie. "What's that?"

"Well, I lead a church group of girls. They're called the ANGELs." She chuckled. "Not that they are, mind you. The purpose of the group is to help others, and this week we are going to be doing some baking for a family. The mother is recovering from surgery. And, well, the girls asked me if you'd be interested in joining us." Alice smiled. "I realize that's a lot to ask. I told them it probably wouldn't work out."

"How old are these girls?" asked Victoria.

"They're preteens," said Alice. "It's a rather lively age, but they're sweet."

"Preteens?" Victoria seemed to be chewing on this. "And this activity is when?"

"Wednesday night." Alice blinked. "In the church basement."

"Oh, why don't you just do it here, Alice," suggested Jane. "My kitchen is much better than the one in the church basement."

"And warmer too," added Louise.

"Yes," agreed Victoria. "And much more photogenic, I'm sure."

"Photogenic?" said Alice, confused.

"Yes." Victoria turned to Cynthia. "You were saying that we need to get some photographs of me doing something with children. I think this is the perfect opportunity."

Cynthia's eyes lit up. "I think you are right. Would it be okay, Aunt Alice?"

"Well, I guess so. I'm sure the girls would be thrilled."

"We'd have to get their parents to sign release forms," said Cynthia as she pulled out her notebook and jotted something down, "but that should be no problem."

"Then it's settled," said Victoria, obviously pleased with herself, "Wednesday night in Jane's kitchen."

"Right," said Alice, wondering what she had got herself into. What had she been thinking, having Victoria and the ANGELs and a photographer—all here in Jane's kitchen? Who knew what could go wrong? She looked at Jane as if searching for backup or a way out, but Jane just smiled at her as if they did things like cook with Victoria Martin every day of the week.

After Victoria had turned in, Cynthia was told the tobacco tea story. They all agreed that Wilhelm was the person to inform her of the secret ingredient if she truly wanted to buy some of his special brew.

"Maybe Victoria is a secret smoker and the tea satisfies her nicotine craving," Jane suggested.

"Or maybe she has absolutely no sense of taste," Cynthia said.

"Maybe she chews," Jane said, warming to the topic.

"*Jane, stop!*" Louise commanded.

Somehow they managed to suppress their giggles as they all tiptoed off to their various bedrooms.

Chapter ❄ Thirteen

A lice was thankful to return to the peaceful routine of work on Monday. *It's funny,* she thought as she drove toward Potterston, *going to work today feels more relaxing than being at home.*

Despite a busy morning, Alice did not forget her commitment to check out the dog-racing track during her lunch hour. She had asked about the track at the hospital, but no one knew much about it since it had only recently opened. Though tempted to relax and put her feet up in the nurses' lounge, instead she bundled up into her heavy wool coat, scarf and gloves, and drove to the address she had found in the phone book. She was not sure what to expect. Still, she felt the need to go—to see this place for herself.

There were no races going on, and the parking lot and stands were almost empty. But there were a number of people and some dogs milling about. She parked on the edge of the lot and tried to look as inconspicuous as possible as she approached what looked like an entrance to the racetrack. She felt certain that someone would stop her, but she managed to walk right through the gate along with several other people. As she entered, what she saw alarmed her. She noticed things like muzzles and tight collars, and a dog with a bad limp that was being picked up and *shoved* into a box, even though he was yelping in pain.

Once inside, she noticed more and more things.

That seemed to flag that all was not well in the world of racing dogs. Oh, some owners seemed genuinely to care about their dogs, but in an area where people were working with their dogs, some people yelled at the animals. One man kicked his. Alice bit her lip and looked away. She continued walking to an area where trucks were parked, not far from the starting gates. Then, turning a corner, she saw a scene that completely horrified her, one that would stay with her for a long, long time. There, stretched out on the frozen grass, were two lifeless dogs. One was a soft golden brown, the other was white with a few chocolate brown spots. Her hand flew to her mouth in revulsion. Just then a large, bearded man appeared with a bright blue plastic tarp.

"What'd'ya think you're doing over here?" he demanded.

She just stood there, speechlessly staring at the two dogs.

The man seemed to soften a little. "Look, lady, I know this don't look good, but both these dogs needed to be put down. It was the humane thing to do, you know."

She shook her head and stepped backward without speaking.

"Let me tell you, lady, there are some folks who wouldn't handle it like this. Some folks would just—" He scowled. "Look, I don't even know why I'm bothering with you. These were *my* dogs, okay? I have a right to do what I want with them. And they weren't no good for anything. *You get it?*" Then he cursed and turned away. Throwing the tarp over them, he began to wrap them up as if they were nothing more than rubbish.

Alice cried tears of outrage as she hurried back to her car. She wished she could wash her hands, although she had touched nothing at the track. She looked at her watch. She still had a half hour before her lunch break would end. She started her engine, and feeling her hands shaking, she drove away from the track and parked at a nearby convenience store. There she took out a pad of paper and furiously began to pen a letter to the editor. Okay, it might not be much, but it was a start. People needed to know about these brutalities. She started her letter with the heading: *Run for Your Life!* Then proceeded to write down what she had just witnessed.

By the time she finished and got back to the hospital, her lunch break was over, but Alice had no appetite anyway. On her next break, she called Carlene Moss at the *Acorn Nutshell.* It was only a small-town paper, but Alice thought that perhaps Carlene would have some ideas about dealing with this deplorable situation. Maybe she would even write an article about it. She quickly explained what had happened and what she had seen.

"You know, I've heard rumors of these things before," said Carlene, "but I'm sorry to say, I have never actually looked into it."

"Well, I wrote what I think could be a letter to the

editor. Is it too late to get it in this week's edition?"

"Can you fax it to me?"

"Sure," said Alice. She could use the fax machine in the nurses' station.

"You get it to me today, and it'll come out on Wednesday," said Carlene.

"Wednesday," said Alice. "That's the same day of the next race. I wonder if I could possibly garner enough interest to get people to come out and stage some kind of a protest."

"I don't know," said Carlene. "Maybe you should wait and let me run a bigger story on it next week."

"Those poor dogs can't wait," said Alice with emotion. "You should have seen them."

"That makes me so mad," said Carlene. "Well, I'm with you, Alice. You go ahead and invite the locals to stage a protest. I might even come myself, if I can get away."

"Right," said Alice. Then she hung up and wrote a few more lines challenging the good people of Acorn Hill to join with her "to take a stand together against the inhumane treatment and cruelty to dogs at the Potterston racetrack." Then she faxed her letter to the number that Carlene had given her.

Although this action was just a beginning, it did make Alice feel a little bit better. At least she was doing *something*. Now, if only she could get those images of the poor dogs out of her head. She really did not want to have nightmares about her experience.

By the time she finished what turned out to be a

demanding shift, she had pushed the greyhound dilemma to the back of her mind. Her hospital work required her full attention. It was not until after she had gone home and cleaned up for dinner that she had time to revisit what had transpired during her lunch hour. Seeing Harold enjoying a congenial visit with Victoria in the living room brought the issue back to her. It was just before dinner, but she could not help herself. "Harold," she said. "I thought you might be interested to know that I visited the racetrack today."

Victoria's eyes widened. "Are you joking, Alice? You don't seem like the track type."

"The racetrack's not open on Mondays," said Harold.

"Maybe not to the general public," said Alice as she sat down in the chair across from them. "But the trainers are there, I guess to prepare the dogs for the next race."

"You're speaking of dog racing?" Victoria's voice was flat.

Alice nodded. "Greyhounds."

"I know what breed of dogs they use to race," said Victoria. "I deplore the practice. In fact, I belong to an organization that campaigns against the sport." She laughed in a sarcastic tone. "If you can call it a sport, that is."

"Wait a minute," said Harold. "I happen to enjoy dog races. I've never seen a single cruel act."

"Well, of course not," snorted Victoria, "they wouldn't show their dark side in public."

"Well, I saw some things today that were not meant for the public," said Alice.

"It's time for dinner," called Louise from the dining room.

Alice now realized this was not the time to discuss such a distasteful issue. As they walked to the dining room, she changed the topic to the weather. "I heard there's a slight chance of snow later this week," she said as everyone took seats at the table.

"Oh, I would love to see some snow," said Jane as she set the soup tureen on the table.

It was Louise's turn to say the blessing. Having guests joining them for dinner was not the norm at Grace Chapel Inn, and Alice had noticed how Victoria had originally seemed to bristle just slightly at their family ritual. Now she appeared to have settled into the routine and simply bowed her head with the rest of them.

"We walked around town a bit today," said Cynthia as the soup was served.

"Oh?" Alice looked up from her bowl, a naughty smile playing on her lips. "Did you visit Time for Tea?"

Cynthia ducked her head to hide her reaction, but Victoria responded, "We did visit the little tea shop. I found Wilhelm Wood to be a perfect dear. I asked him to make me up a special batch of his new signature tea."

"Signature tea?" Louise's eyebrow lifted.

"Yes." Victoria nodded. "I told him I would have it

111

tested for possible inclusion in the Victoria Line."

Jane's eyes were sparkling when she asked, "And was Wilhelm happy about that?"

"In fact, he seemed somewhat taken aback. He's a very dignified fellow," said Victoria, "which I can certainly appreciate. I was grateful he didn't become giddy the way some people do."

"Giddy . . ." repeated Louise while giving Jane a warning look. "No, I am sure that Wilhelm controlled his . . . joy at the news."

Alice and her sisters, of course, knew why he had seemed so controlled. How embarrassing it would be for Wilhelm, a man who loved fine tea, to have his name attached to this "signature" tea that was really just a horrible and foul-tasting mistake. Alice wondered if he had revealed the secret ingredient yet. It did not seem as if he had.

Harold could tell something was going on, but he knew better than to ask about it in front of Victoria. Soon the subject changed to the other shops in town. It seemed that Victoria had approved of both Craig Tracy's flower shop and Sylvia Songer's fabric shop.

"I found several pieces of vintage cloth at Sylvia's Buttons," said Victoria. "I don't think the owner had any idea as to the value because I got them for a song." Victoria laughed.

"Oh, Sylvia knows the old pieces are valuable," said Jane, "but there aren't many people in Acorn Hill who can afford such things. I'm sure she was honored to have you in her shop."

"It's funny, isn't it?" said Victoria. "That happens to me all the time. People *give* me merchandise or *reduce* the price on items, and I, of all people, could certainly afford to pay more." She laughed again. "I'm not complaining, mind you."

"How's the book coming?" asked Alice, once again eager to change the subject since she thought she noticed faint sparks flashing in Jane's eyes.

"Oh, don't ask," said Victoria.

Cynthia shook her head. "It's not coming too well." She glanced at Victoria. "*We* keep changing our minds."

"And it's due the end of the week?" asked Jane.

"Something like that," said Cynthia.

Alice felt sorry for her niece. Not only did she look completely discouraged, but she also had dark circles under her eyes. "Is there anything we can do to help?" she asked.

Cynthia shook her head. "You are doing plenty. We're the ones who need to get our act together."

"Perhaps we should start earlier tomorrow," offered Victoria. "I have no problem working before breakfast."

"Yes, that might be a good idea," agreed Cynthia. "In that case, I may turn in early tonight. Also, I need to go over today's notes to see if I can figure something out."

"Goodness," said Louise. "I had no idea that writing a children's book was so challenging."

Cynthia laughed. "That's what most people think.

You have no idea how many people come to me—people who have never published a single word—and tell me that they think they will write a children's book. They think it should be easy."

"Why is it so difficult?" asked Alice.

"Well, you're writing a complete story with a beginning, a middle, and an end. You need a strong character, a good plot, and it has to be about something children care about. And you have to do all this in a minimum of words. It's very tricky."

"And then you have to consider the art," said Jane.

"Yes." Cynthia nodded enthusiastically. "You must write each spread—that's like how the book looks when it's open in your lap—as a specific scene that lends itself to illustration. Also, you want each spread to be different. Believe me, it's not all that easy."

"I have to agree with her," said Victoria. "I came here thinking it would be a snap." She sighed. "Unfortunately it's turning out to be quite overwhelming."

Cynthia reached over and patted Victoria's hand. "Don't worry, we're going to nail this thing by the end of the week."

"I certainly hope so." Victoria looked surprisingly serious just then. "I really despise failing at *anything*."

"I know how you feel," said Cynthia.

Poor Cynthia, thought Alice, *has much more at stake with this book than Victoria.* "I will be praying for you both," she said. "I will make it the top of my prayer list for each day."

Victoria looked stunned. "You pray every single day?"

Alice smiled. "Actually, I pray off and on throughout the day." She shrugged. "It's very comforting, really, just talking to God."

"Talking to God?" Victoria looked unconvinced. "Does He listen?"

Alice laughed. "I believe He does. My prayers are always answered."

Now Victoria looked quite skeptical. "Always? That's hard to believe."

"Always," said Alice in a firm voice. "Of course, I don't always like His answers. Sometimes He says 'no,' but many times He goes beyond what I could imagine."

"I can vouch for that," said Jane. "I wasn't much into prayer before I moved back home. That's been steadily changing."

"Interesting," said Harold. It was almost the first word he had spoken during the meal. Perhaps it was hard getting a word in edgewise with five chatty ladies at the table. "My wife became a firm believer in prayer during the last few years of her life."

"That must have been a comfort to her," said Louise.

"Oh, it was." He nodded thoughtfully. "And, oddly enough, it was a comfort to me, too. I guess that was because in some ways she seemed much more at peace with her situation than I was. Of course, everything changed once she was gone."

"I have discovered," said Louise, "that things like prayer and faith must be worked out on an individual basis."

"I agree," said Jane. "Even though our father was a pastor, each of his three daughters had to come to her belief in an individual way."

"And at an individual time," added Alice.

"That's because God is infinitely creative," said Jane. "He didn't make any of us alike."

"That's true enough," said Harold. "Once again, you ladies have given me something—well, besides this lovely dinner—to chew on."

Chapter ❄ Fourteen

While Cynthia and Victoria worked, Louise was at a book club meeting, and Jane was attending Sylvia's quilting class. Alice sat at the dining room table making protest signs. Harold came upon her sitting there with pieces of poster board and felt pens spread out across the table.

"You're really taking this seriously?" he said as he looked over her shoulder.

She nodded as she carefully filled in the block letter with a black felt pen.

"STOP CRUELTY TO INNOCENT DOGS," read Harold. "*Hmmm.*"

"Well, it's not the snappiest line," said Alice, "but it's the best I can do at the moment."

"Why are you making so many of them?" he asked.

"Because I expect to be joined by others," she explained without looking up. "I said I'd bring the signs."

"Have you ever done anything like this before?"

"Well, no, but there's a first time for everything." Alice felt unsure now. Maybe this was a crazy idea after all. She had not had the opportunity to describe to Harold what she had seen at the track on Monday. Taking a break from her sign-making, she stood up and looked the old man in the eye. "I never told you about the scene at the racetrack, Harold, about what I saw on Monday during my lunch break."

"Well, no, you didn't say much about it."

"I saw two dead dogs, Harold."

His brow creased slightly. "How did they die?"

"I don't know for sure, but it didn't look good."

He shook his head. "I'm sure it didn't. But perhaps these dogs needed to be put down for a good reason."

"That's what their owner said."

"So?"

"Well, that wasn't all. Trainers were yelling at their dogs and hitting them."

He nodded. "I don't know much about training animals, but that doesn't sound too terrible to me."

"And the dogs are kept in these tiny boxes." She held up her hands to show the dimensions.

He nodded again. "How do you know the dogs don't like it in there?"

"Because one poor dog was yelping as he was stuffed into his." Alice sighed in frustration. It seemed obvious that Harold was not sympathetic to her cause. He went into the kitchen and returned with a cup of coffee.

"I'm not saying you're wrong, Alice," he said in a kind voice. "I don't agree with cruelty to animals either. But it's possible that you're overreacting."

She considered this, then finally said, "It's possible, Harold, but I really don't think I am."

"Well, I wish you the best tomorrow." He winked at her. "Maybe I'll head out to the track myself."

She started to feel hopeful, but then realized he would probably be up in the stands cheering for whichever dog he had bet on.

The next morning, Alice stopped by the Coffee Shop to pick up the new edition of the *Acorn Nutshell* on her way to work.

"Eager to read the local news, Alice?" called Hope from behind the counter.

Alice smiled. "Actually, I wrote a letter to the editor. I'm hoping it made it in here today."

Hope filled Ronald Simpson's coffee cup. "I'll have to read it when I have time." She rolled her eyes as Chuck Parker waved his cup at her. "Which might not be until next March."

"Sooner than that, I hope," called Alice as she went back outside.

Alice opened the paper when she got into her car. There at the top of the "Editor's Mailbag" was her letter, with the heading in large type: RUN FOR YOUR LIFE! She was embarrassed as she read what she had written so hastily and with such passion. Of course, it was true, but it did not sound like her. She wondered what her friends and neighbors would think; however, she had little time to worry about that now. She started the car and drove to the hospital, which she found was busier than usual with several unscheduled surgeries and three nurses out with the flu. As a result, she worked right through her lunch break and it was two-thirty before she was reminded of her plans for the day.

"I thought you were taking off early today," said her supervisor.

Alice looked at her watch. "I guess I lost track of the time."

"Well, things seem to have finally settled down, and I noticed you missed your lunch break. Feel free to leave whenever you need to, Alice."

"Thanks." Within minutes she was bundled up, in her car, and nervously driving toward the racetrack. Her heart pounded as her car neared the track. She had never done anything like this in her entire life and was not sure she could do it now. She could tell by the parking lot that there had to be a good-sized crowd expected. That was encouraging: Perhaps the presence of her and her friends would make these people think twice about what they had previously considered "innocent fun."

In her letter in the *Nutshell*, she had invited interested parties to meet her at the main entrance. She had also spoken individually with several people, including her sisters and her best friend Vera Humbert. All had promised, a few somewhat reluctantly, to arrive around three when the final segment of races would be run.

When Alice reached the main entrance, laden with her cumbersome pile of homemade signs, she saw not a single soul that she recognized. She paced back and forth for a bit, searching the faces in the crowd and silently praying that God would show her what to do next. And finally, sticking the other signs back in her trunk, she selected one that read, "DOG ABUSE IS NOT A SPORT."

Then, holding it up in front of her, she planted herself next to the front entrance and waited.

She could feel her blood pressure rise as the first group of people approached. It consisted of three middle-aged men and a younger woman. At first they looked at her curiously, perhaps feeling sorry for the old woman in the heavy wool coat. Upon reading the sign, however, their countenances changed, and one of the men made a rude and unrepeatable comment.

"Get a life," snapped the young woman as she pulled her fur coat more tightly around her and strutted past.

Next came two men, probably in their thirties. Bracing herself, she held up her sign so that they could easily read it.

"Aw, come on," said one. "Give us a break."

"Yeah, you 'PITA PETA' people need to lighten up."

On it went. Feeling that she was doing her duty,

Alice persevered, but the temperature was dropping steadily, and despite her hat, gloves and scarf, she was getting very cold. Then a few snowflakes began to fly. Finally, she decided that everyone who was coming to the races was already inside, and ready to give it up, she started to leave. Just then people started drifting back out. Torn between wanting to be warm—not to mention ending what was probably the most unusual thing she had ever attempted—and feeling her responsibility to make a statement, she decided to remain a bit longer. Perhaps Vera would come after all. Or maybe her sisters. She glanced at the clock above the entrance. It was just a little past four now. Certainly she could give this protest more than an hour of her time. Besides, she noticed, people were coming out in greater numbers now. It seemed that they too were getting cold.

What Alice had not counted on was that many of these people were not only cold and grumpy (after losing their bets, she suspected), but also had been imbibing. What had started out as a handful of rude remarks and jibes was quickly becoming more personal and threatening.

Dear God, she prayed silently as a group of angry spectators clustered around her, *help me through this.*

"Stay out of what you don't understand!" yelled an angry man with alcohol on his breath.

"Go home, old woman!" This came from a man only inches from her face.

Alice simply closed her eyes and held up her sign,

praying all the while. The voices continued their assault, but the specific words became blurred in her ears as she silently repeated Psalm 23 in her head.

A bright flash of light caused her to open her eyes. Standing in front of her, snapping pictures, was a young man. He had his camera focused on her and the angry crowd, which had grown surprisingly large. Toward the back of the crowd was Carlene. Then Alice heard, "Break it up! Break it up!" and saw police moving toward her. She was not sure whether to be thankful or frightened.

"Alice!" called Harold, waving frantically from the sidelines. "You need some help?"

She never had a chance to answer.

"What's going on here, ma'am?" demanded an officer.

"I was protesting," she began.

"Did you know this is private property?" he asked her.

"Well, no."

"The owner of the property has made a complaint," he told her. "We have to take you in."

"You're going to arrest me?"

"That's right."

Now she was feeling slightly faint. She searched through the dispersing crowd, hunting for Harold or Carlene. Finally she spotted them. Both were trying to press their way through.

"Excuse me," called Harold, waving to the police. "I'm with the lady."

"Let him through," yelled an officer.

"Let me through!" yelled Carlene. "I'm the press."

Soon both Carlene and Harold were standing nearby, and Alice felt slightly better, though decidedly light-headed. She hoped she was not about to faint.

"May I escort the lady home?" offered Harold in his most charming manner.

"Sorry," said the officer. "She's going downtown."

"Downtown?" repeated Carlene. "You mean you're arresting her?"

"That's right," said the officer. He looked from Harold to Carlene. "Are you people involved in this protest too?"

Harold shook his head.

"I'm a reporter," said Carlene.

"Do you really need to arrest her?" asked Harold. "I can vouch that this woman is interested only in peaceful protest."

"Has nothing to do with it." The officer turned his attention back to Alice now. "You want to come quietly, little lady?"

She nodded and handed him her sign. "Are you going to handcuff me?" she asked in a voice that was barely audible.

"Nah, I don't think that'll be necessary." Now he actually smiled at her. "Just come along, okay?"

She nodded again and began walking with the policemen toward their cars. She was surprised to see the blue lights flashing, amazed that they had gone to all this trouble on account of her and her protest. When they reached the car, the officer introduced himself to her as Sergeant Crane, and then wrote down her full name, address, Social Security number and birth date in his little book.

"I'll let your sisters know, Alice," called Harold from nearby.

"Don't worry, Alice," called Carlene. "They won't be able to hold you for long."

Snowflakes were flying faster now, and Alice watched them numbly as she rode in the backseat of the squad car—like a criminal. They were now passing the hospital where she had worked for years as a respected head nurse. There was Ron White scraping snow off the windows of his old dented pickup. She started to wave but then thought better of it. With a sinking heart, she watched the snowflakes zipping past the side window as the car continued toward town. Oh, what had she gotten herself into?

It was getting dusky when they reached the police station in downtown Potterston. They did not park in front as she had expected, but went down a narrow alley where they took her into a side door that appeared to be close to the city jail.

"Are you going to lock me up?" she asked as she glanced at the security gates in the hallway that she felt certain led to the jail. She wondered what it would be like in one of those cells, and whether or not she would have to spend the night.

"We'll see," said Sergeant Crane.

First, he filled out some preliminary paperwork, and then took her to where a stern-looking woman took her photograph and copies of her fingerprints. Alice did not know when she had felt so foolish and humiliated. She considered trying to explain her dilemma to the tight-lipped woman but decided it was probably not worth the effort. After what seemed like an hour, Sergeant Crane finally led her to his office.

"Alice," called Harold from the waiting area.

"He your husband?" asked the sergeant.

"No, just a friend."

"Do you want him to join us?"

"Could he?" asked Alice hopefully. She and Harold might not see everything eye-to-eye, but he was certainly better than no one right now.

"Sure." Sergeant Crane called out to Harold. "Care to join us?"

Alice was surprised at how comforting it was to have Harold sitting next to her in Sergeant Crane's little office.

Harold reached over and squeezed her gloved hand as the sergeant turned on his computer and waited for the screen to warm up. "Don't worry," said the sergeant. "I'm sure we'll have you out of here in no time."

"Did you call my sisters yet?" she asked Harold with some uncertainty. She was not sure how eager she was to have them knowing her whereabouts.

"I haven't had a chance yet. Do you want me to do that now?"

"*Nooo*," she said slowly, "maybe not yet. I know Jane will be busy with dinner and—"

"Okay," interrupted the sergeant. "I need to ask a few more questions and run this through the computer."

So, for what seemed like a long time, she answered questions and waited while the sergeant went to attend to some other, obviously more pressing, matter.

Alice looked at her watch. "Goodness, it's six-thirty," she said. She turned to Harold. "Perhaps you'd better call my sisters now. They may be worried."

"Right." He nodded. "There's a pay phone in the lobby." He had just left when Alice realized that tonight was the ANGELs meeting and that the girls had planned to meet at the inn for their baking project, the project that Victoria was planning to participate in. *Good grief,* she thought, *could things get any worse?*

Soon Harold returned. "You're right, they were worried. I spoke with Louise."

"What did she say?"

"As you can imagine she was quite stunned by the news." He smiled.

Alice *could* imagine.

"I told her that if all went well, we'd have you home in no time."

She shook her head, swallowing against the lump now forming in her throat. "I don't know about that." A tear trickled down her cheek.

Harold pulled a clean white handkerchief from his pocket and handed it to her. "Oh, come now, Alice. This isn't so had, really."

"I know." She nodded and wiped her eyes. "It's just . . . I feel so . . . so stupid. I don't know why I decided to take on this thing. I mean, it seemed right at the time. But, really, this is just so unlike me."

He patted her hand. "Well, I've got a little confession to make, Alice."

She looked up at him in surprise.

"I decided to come out to the track early today. Just to look around, you know. After the things you'd said, well, I was curious." He cleared his throat. "I wandered over to the area where the trucks all park and they keep the dogs, back where the public isn't really supposed to be." He shook his head. "Well."

"Did you see something?"

He nodded sadly. "I saw a couple of things that made me realize this wasn't the kind of sport I want to support. I waited around for you until almost three o'clock, but I was so cold by then that I went into the concessions and got some coffee. Then, I met an old friend from my days in the service and we got to talking. Well, by the time I came back outside, there you were getting mobbed by the crazies."

Just then the sergeant came back. "Sorry to keep you, Miss Howard."

"That's all right." She forced a tiny smile to her lips.

"Well, let me run this now and see if you're wanted in any other states." He chuckled. "Not that we think you are. Your record is as clean as a whistle, Miss Howard. And I have good news. I called the track owner and he agreed not to press charges. However, you may not step on the property again."

Alice gave a smile and waited patiently. It was half

past seven by the time she was released. She took a moment to phone home, concerned about what might be going on in Jane's kitchen with her ANGELs and Victoria Martin.

"Don't worry," Jane assured her. "Everything is under control."

"You sound a little stressed," said Alice.

Jane laughed. "You should talk, sister."

"What a day!" said Alice.

"You're telling me." Jane sighed. "We'll have a lot to talk about when you get here."

"Please, give my girls my apologies."

"Don't worry. We already did. They think you're a local hero now for saving the dogs."

"I didn't save anything," said Alice with disappointment.

"Watch out with that!" Jane suddenly yelped.

"Is everything okay?" asked Alice.

"Ashley's got her pigtail stuck in my Cuisinart," said Jane quickly. "Gotta go!"

Chapter ❄ Fifteen

I have to pick up my car," Alice told Harold as they pulled away from the police station. Fortunately, it had stopped snowing, at least for the moment.

"No problem," said Harold as he turned up his heater. "I don't recall seeing any security gates at the racetrack. We should be able to go right in and get your car." He glanced at her as they stopped at the red light. "Are you sure you're able to drive? You've had quite an afternoon."

"I should get it tonight," she said. "Just in case the snow is worse tomorrow."

"Do you work tomorrow?" he asked as he pulled into the parking lot at the track.

"My part-time workweek ended today," she told him. "Thank goodness. I usually work a half-day on Thursday, but I decided to take some vacation hours tomorrow."

He parked next to her car, then got out and helped her to scrape off the snow. "I'll follow you home," he said.

"Oh, I forgot," she said suddenly. "You don't like to drive after dark."

His grin showed up in his headlights. "Well, I figure if you can stand up to the racing fans and get yourself arrested and nearly thrown in jail, I should be able to drive back to Acorn Hill."

"We'll take it slowly," she promised. "The roads will be slick."

Alice kept a vigilant eye on the pair of headlights that followed her. She also prayed that God would get them both home safely as well as watch over whatever might be going on in Jane's kitchen.

By the time she parked her car in front of the inn, she felt as if she had been through a war. The little digital clock in her car said it was eight-thirty, and she knew that was about the time when the ANGELs would normally be cleaning up. But nothing felt normal about this day.

"How are you doing?" she asked Harold as she waited for him to climb out of his car.

"Not too bad," he said as he walked over to her. "You know what?"

"What?" she asked as they walked up the front walk, their feet making crunching noises in the freshly fallen snow.

"Driving in the snow and the dark reminded me of back when I was flying reconnaissance during the war."

"Really?" she turned and peered at his face in the porch light.

He was beaming. "Yes, I actually found it invigorating and exciting."

She opened the door to the sounds of many voices. "My girls group is here tonight," she warned him. "You may want to make yourself scarce."

"Not on your life," he said as he removed his overcoat. "I'm just starting to like all this craziness."

"Miss Howard!" shrieked Ashley who had heard the front door open and had come to investigate. "They let you out of jail."

Soon all her ANGELs were in the front hall clustered around her, hugging her and acting as if she had just survived a life-threatening experience.

"Did they really lock you up?" asked Jenny with wide eyes.

"Did you ride in a police car?" asked Sissy.

"Did you need a lawyer?" asked Linda.

"Slow down," said Alice as she quickly filled them

130

in on the most basic details. "Now, I want to know what you girls have been up to. Last I heard, it sounded as if things were out of control in my sister's kitchen."

Alice pushed open the swinging doors and frowned. "This doesn't look good," she said to no one in particular.

"It's not our fault, Miss Howard," claimed Sissy. "It's Miss Martin who kept messing things up."

"*Miss Martin?*" Alice looked skeptically at her less-than-angelic ANGELs.

"That's the truth," said Jane as she emerged from the laundry room.

"Honestly," said Ashley as she twirled a pigtail that was coated with something like batter. "She's the messiest cook we've ever seen. She spilled flour and sugar all over the counters when she was measuring. Then she let three eggs roll off the counter and smash on the floor."

"Well, she is used to lots of helpers to measure and clean up," said Jane, unable to hide the satisfaction in her voice even as she made excuses for Victoria.

"Miss Martin isn't a very good baker," said Jenny in a quiet voice. "None of her things turned out right."

"Where is Miss Martin?" asked Alice with concern.

"She went to bed with a headache," said Ashley. "My mom does that a lot too, especially when I have friends over."

"Did we get any baking done for the Meads?" asked Alice.

"Oh yeah," said Jenny.

The girls pulled Alice over to the counter where a number of interesting items were cooling, taking time to point out which things they had helped to create.

"And there's still some things in the oven," said Sissy with pride.

Alice glanced at Jane, certain that any successes were a result of her sister's generous help. "Did you all tell Ms. Howard thank you?"

"Thank you, Ms. Howard," they all chanted.

To Alice's relief, the parents began to arrive to pick up their girls. Once the house had quieted down, Alice asked Harold if he was as hungry as she was.

"You two just sit down right here," said Jane, pointing to the kitchen table. "You tell me what happened at the race-track while I warm up your dinners."

"Don't start without me," called Louise as she hurried into the kitchen. "I want to hear every word."

Alice and Harold recapped the story. Alice filled in the facts and Harold added the drama, and by the time they finished their late supper, Alice's story was told.

"My goodness," said Louise.

"We wanted to come," said Jane. "But then I heard that Victoria had arranged for a camera crew to be in my kitchen." She shook her head. "Well, I felt I had to get things in order."

Louise laughed as she waved her arm around the incredibly messy kitchen. "As if that mattered, Jane."

Jane rolled her eyes.

"I would have come," said Louise, "but it had started to snow over here, and you know how I hate driving on snow."

"Vera called," said Jane, "and said they had an emergency meeting at the school because of an outbreak of lice."

"*Ugh,*" said Louise.

"Some of the ANGELs go to Vera's school," said Alice.

"Yes," said Jane, "but Vera said the outbreak was limited to the lower grades."

"Thank goodness," sighed Louise. "Just the thought makes me feel itchy."

Harold laughed. "Life never seems to slow down for you ladies." He stood up and saluted them. "Good night all."

"Was Cynthia down here for the baking project?" asked Alice.

"No, thank goodness," said Louise. "The poor girl was in her room trying to make heads or tails of what she and Victoria worked on today. It does not sound as if the book is coming along too well."

"And the week's almost over," said Alice.

"Just halfway," said Jane.

"Feels to me as though it should be over," said Louise in a weary voice.

Then they all said good night and went quietly up the stairs to their rooms, with hopes of enjoying long winter's nap.

Chapter ❄ Sixteen

I heard about your little adventure yesterday," said Victoria when Alice came into the dining room for breakfast.

Alice forced a smile as she poured herself a cup of tea. "Yes, it was a rather startling day."

"Is that Alice?" called Jane as she emerged from the kitchen with a platter of tempting cheese blintzes.

"Sorry," said Alice, "I didn't mean to sleep so late."

Jane set the platter next to a bowl of shiny golden peaches that Alice knew Jane had canned herself last summer. "That's not it," said Jane. "I've just been dying to tell you what I discovered last night."

"Last night?" Alice felt confused.

"Yes." Jane sat down and poured herself a cup of coffee. "I couldn't sleep, and I decided to do some research online about greyhound racing."

"Everyone's getting into the act," said Harold as he lowered his newspaper.

"Well, maybe it's about time," said Jane. "The things I read and saw about the mistreatment of greyhounds made me absolutely sick. I even printed a few things out for you to read, Alice. Although I'd suggest you have your breakfast first."

"I wish you'd have let me know that you were ⸱ging a protest yesterday," said Victoria. "I might've ⸱ able to help you."

⸱lly?" Alice peered over her teacup at Victoria.

134

"Well, I'm sure Cynthia wouldn't have allowed me to attend it since we haven't made too much progress on the book yet." Victoria scowled. "But I might've been able to get you some publicity."

Alice frowned. "I'm not sure that would've helped much. I'm afraid I didn't make much of an impact standing there all by myself and holding up my one little sign."

"You made enough of an impact to get yourself arrested," said Jane. "That's nothing to sneeze at."

Alice smiled. "I guess not. To be honest, if I'd known that I was going to end up being fingerprinted at the Potterston police station, I might've reconsidered the whole thing from the start."

"I think you just went about it all wrong," said Victoria as she pushed away her now empty plate.

"I'm sure I did," agreed Alice, not eager to be lectured by this woman who apparently considered herself to be an expert on all things—all things other than baking projects with giggling preteen girls. The thought made Alice smile.

"What you failed to do was plan," continued Victoria without noticing Alice's reaction. "You know what they say you should do when you fail to plan."

"Plan to fail," offered Alice automatically. This was something a certain hospital administrator liked to say repeatedly at work, not to Alice, of course, but she used that line on many of the more inexperienced nurses and aides.

"That's right," said Victoria. She glanced over at Cynthia now. "How firm is our book deadline, Cynthia?"

Cynthia's eyes widened. "It's pretty firm, Victoria."

"What if I spoke to Edward," said Victoria in a suddenly sweet voice. "What if I pleaded and begged him to give us just a few more days?"

"Why would you do that?" Cynthia's expression was a mix of confusion and exasperation.

"So that I could help your aunt with her greyhound protest."

Cynthia glanced at Alice. "Do you want help, Aunt Alice?"

Alice was at a loss for words. The truth was she wanted to put this whole thing far, far behind her. "I— *uh*—I'm not sure."

"Oh, it's perfectly understandable that you should feel discouraged, Alice," said Victoria. "You meant well, but it went wrong."

"What are you suggesting, Victoria?" asked Jane.

"I think Alice should let me contact my friends and my connections, and we should all help her to stage another protest. A protest during which no one gets arrested, but which gets national press coverage."

"National press coverage?" repeated Alice, her interest now growing.

"Of course." Victoria sat up straighter. "Whenever you attach the name of Victoria Martin to a cause, you can be assured of national press coverage. Now what days do they have races?"

"The next race days are Friday and Saturday," offered Harold.

"Well, Friday is too soon, but Saturday work," said Victoria. "If I get on the phone morning and get the wheels rolling."

"You'd do all that for me?" asked Alice in a me voice.

Victoria cleared her throat. "Nothing personal, Alice, but I'd do *all that* for the dogs."

Alice nodded, feeling embarrassed. "Of course, that's what I meant."

Victoria smiled now. "Then it's settled?"

"Well, wait a minute," said Cynthia. "Nothing is settled until you get Mr. Wentworth to agree to delaying our deadline."

Victoria smiled. "No problem. Just leave Edward to me."

As usual, Victoria was right. By mid-morning her short phone call to the publisher had secured them five additional days to finish the book.

"Oh, Aunt Alice," said Cynthia as she told her mother and aunts the news. "I don't know whether to thank you or to scream."

"I'm sorry," said Alice.

"I'm with Cynthia," said Louise. "I do not know whether we should be happy or go pull our hair out. Do you realize that your greyhound protest means we must put up with Victoria Martin for five more days?"

"Hey," said Jane. "I'm the one who should be complaining the most."

"I'm sorry, Jane." Alice wondered what she could do to make it up to them.

okay, Alice," said Jane. "After reading up on poor dogs last night, I can see why you're coned. I plan to help with the protest for sure."

"I want to help too," said Louise.

"I still have signs," said Alice hopefully.

"Maybe we can liven them up," offered Jane.

"Of course," said Alice. "You're the artist."

"Actually, I was thinking more about using some of the photos I found on the Web site. I could print them out on the printer. Maybe blow some of them up."

"If you don't mind, I'll stay home and work," said Cynthia. "Maybe I'll get more done without Victoria."

"That's fine, dear. I'll call Vera and a few others and make sure we get a good showing," said Alice.

"Maybe I should pack a picnic lunch and some hot beverages," suggested Jane.

"Do the dogs race in weather like this?" asked Louise. "We've got an inch of snow on the ground."

"According to what I read last night, they do," said Jane. "I read one story about how owners make their dogs run in such low temperatures that they get frost-bitten feet and are killed because of it. They also suffer from heat strokes when it's hot out. It can be a cruel sport."

"Even Harold is starting to agree with us," said Alice as she relayed his experience at the track yesterday.

"Well, Alice," said Louise. "It looks like you've really started something here."

"I didn't start it," said Alice.

"But you're starting to get it noticed," said L... "And that's what counts."

Before the day was over, Alice had enlisted all kin... of support for her cause, from Carlene, who had bee... talking to everyone in town, to Vera, who had her fifth graders write letters and make posters and was considering a "field trip" to help with the protest. Even Alice's ANGELs were on board.

"My mom said she'll take a load of us in her van," said Ashley Moore when she called Alice that evening. "Just tell us when and where."

It was settled. Saturday at noon, the protesters would converge on public property, the sides of the street that led to the racetrack. The first race would not begin until one, but this would give them a chance to target the dog owners.

"I realize that not all greyhound owners are cruel to their dogs," said Alice at dinner, "but I think the good ones should take some responsibility here too."

"That's right," said Victoria. "If responsible owners know of cases of mistreatment, they should be required to report them." Then she went on to tell about all the contacts she had made and who would be attending the protest.

Suddenly Alice felt bad for Jane. She had made a perfectly lovely meal, but it seemed that talk of greyhounds was taking over and casting a negative light on everything. Alice decided to try to change the subject. "Did you manage to get any good photos last night, Victoria?" she asked.

…ctoria's laughter had an edge of sarcasm to it. …ell, that remains to be seen." She exhaled loudly. "I …ppose you heard what a fiasco that became, Alice."

"I heard it got a little crazy."

"I occasionally have children on my television show," said Victoria, "but it's always within a very calm and controlled environment. And, of course, we're never broadcasting live. We can always go back and edit our tapes and delete anything that doesn't work."

Alice chuckled. "Sometimes I wish life was like that."

"I'm with you," agreed Jane.

"Your girls, Alice, are a lively bunch, but I haven't the foggiest idea why you call them angels," said Victoria. "If you ask me, they are really a bunch of little devils."

Alice smiled. "Actually, ANGELs is an acronym."

"For what?" asked Victoria.

"Sorry, but you'd have to be an ANGEL to know that. Speaking of ANGELs," continued Alice, "they'll be joining us at the racetrack on Saturday."

"I suppose it wouldn't hurt to have some children present," said Victoria.

"Speaking of children," said Cynthia, "do you think we could spend a couple of hours on the book this evening, Victoria?"

Victoria shrugged. "If you think it's necessary."

Cynthia looked like she was a pot that was close to boiling over. "I think so," she said in a tight voice.

As promised, Alice had been praying for the pair of them on a daily basis. She had been asking God to give them some sort of divine inspiration that would not only rescue Cynthia's job, but also lead to a wonderful book for children. Now she had a feeling she was asking for a real miracle.

Chapter ❄ Seventeen

"Oh my," said Jane on Friday morning as she and Alice fixed breakfast. "With all that's been going on with the dog-racing protest, I have completely forgotten about our sing-along tomorrow night."

"Oh dear," said Alice. "I'm afraid I did too. That'll be an awfully busy day. Have you already invited people?"

"Yes. To be honest, I wish we could postpone it to when Victoria is gone, but Cynthia is looking forward to it."

"Victoria still rubbing you wrong?"

Jane shrugged. "It's hard not to let that woman get to me."

"It's nice how she's helping with the protest."

"I suppose so, although I suspect it's mostly self-serving."

"You don't think she cares about the dogs?"

"Maybe, but I doubt that she would involve herself if she didn't think it would improve her public image. Cynthia said that's why she's doing the children's book."

Alice finished squeezing the oranges that Jane had set out for juice. "Well, just the same, maybe it's good for Victoria."

"You mean to humanize her?"

Alice chuckled as she remembered how humble and human the protest had made her feel. "It couldn't hurt."

"I don't know," said Jane as she flipped a pancake. "With all her cameras and media people clustering around, she might just enjoy all the attention."

"Those cameras and media people will be good for the dogs."

Jane smiled. "As usual, you're probably right."

"Oh, Jane," said Alice. "I wish you wouldn't say that all the time." Then she described, in more detail, some of the things she had experienced on Wednesday.

"Good grief," said Jane as she piled the pancakes on the already warmed plate. "That must've been awful."

"It was one of my worst moments," said Alice. "Believe me, I was questioning myself even more than the police were. If Harold hadn't shown up when he did, I'm sure I would've just crumbled and sobbed."

"Poor Alice," said Jane as she patted her sister's back.

"You know what helped me to get through it, Jane?" Alice now lowered her voice because she thought she heard someone in the dining room. "I thought about all the Bible heroes who had been persecuted for doing the right thing. I thought if they could endure what they went through, surely I could put up with a little discomfort and humiliation for those poor, helpless animals. Of course, compared to those of the Bible heroes, my cause was fairly insignificant."

"Well, I'm proud of you," said Jane.

After breakfast, Alice took time to write Mark Graves a letter. She knew that he would enjoy hearing about her effort—even if somewhat haphazard and ill-planned—in staging her first animal-protection protest. For Mark's sake, she took a more humorous approach as she described her detention at the police station. Then she decided to leave her letter unfinished until after Saturday's event. No one could know how that would turn out.

Since Jane insisted on carrying on with her sing-along party, and Louise planned to spend the morning getting groceries and running errands, Alice rolled up her sleeves and recruited herself as Jane's number one KP person. "At your service," she told Jane with a mock salute.

Jane's plan was to prepare everything ahead of time. "Just in case we don't get back when we expect," said Jane.

"Oh, I think we should easily be back here by mid-afternoon," Alice assured her.

"Yes, but last time you thought you'd be back in time for ANGELs," Jane reminded her.

"Don't worry, I'm sure we won't end up in jail," said Alice, inwardly shuddering at the thought of a second arrest within the same week. If the police took her in again, they would probably lock her up.

"Well, I'd just rather have everything ready," said Jane.

"I think that's smart," agreed Alice. "I hope you'll feel free to leave the protest early if necessary."

"Yes, I might do that."

"*Yoo-hoo,*" called Ethel from the back porch as she let herself in.

"Hey, Aunt Ethel," said Jane. "Did you come over to see our jailbird in person?"

"I heard all about it," said Ethel. "Our Alice is the talk of the town." Now she peered at Alice as if she thought the experience might have changed something about her. "Are you okay, Alice?"

Alice laughed. "Of course, I'm okay. I'll admit it did shake me up some. I was just telling Jane if Harold hadn't been there to bail me out—"

"He had to *bail* you out?"

"Well, not literally. He was just there to lend moral support, which I badly needed at the time." Alice paused. "Speaking of Harold?"

Ethel smiled. "Don't trouble yourself, Alice. Lloyd and I are working it all out."

"Good."

"In fact, I think I almost have him talked into escorting me to Jane's little party tomorrow night." She looked at Jane now. "It's still on, isn't it? I heard that half the town is planning some kind of march at the Potterston racetrack Saturday."

"At least half," said Jane, "but the party is still on."

"Oh good." Ethel clapped her hands. "I'm already working on outfits for Lloyd and me."

"What are they?" asked Jane.

"Top secret," said Ethel. "Need any help in here, girls?"

Soon Ethel was working with them and it did not take too long before Jane convinced her aunt to do her civic duty and attend the protest with them.

"I suppose I could go," said Ethel. "Lloyd was considering it, although he was a bit concerned about taking a political position on something like this."

"A political position?" asked Alice.

"Well, you know," said Ethel. "He was telling me that this whole animal-rights thing is very divisive among constituents."

"In Acorn Hill?" Alice was skeptical.

"Don't you remember the flap over Clara Horn's pig?"

Alice laughed. "That hardly seemed an animal-rights issue. Besides, I'd think the citizens of Acorn Hill would appreciate their mayor taking a stand against this kind of outrageous animal abuse."

"Yes, you're probably right, dear."

Just then, Cynthia burst through the swinging door. "It's useless," she said as she shook her head and helped herself to a gingersnap still warm from the oven. "That woman is totally insane."

"What's wrong now?" asked Jane as she wiped her hands on her apron and poured Cynthia a cup of coffee.

"She just doesn't get it," said Cynthia as she sank into a kitchen chair. "We were almost getting some-

where today. We decided to create this character, a little beaver that, of course, she wants to call Bucky."

"That's cute," said Ethel.

Cynthia frowned at her great aunt. "Cute, maybe, but not very original."

"Oh."

"But anyway, we're really starting to cook on this Bucky Beaver when Victoria suddenly suggests that we turn him into an otter. So, I'm trying to work with her, and I agree, but when I suggest we should consider another name, she won't budge. No,' she tells me in her I'm-the-boss tone, 'this is going to be Bucky Otter.' Cynthia shook her head. "Bucky Otter!"

Jane and Alice laughed, but Ethel seemed to think that Bucky Otter was just fine.

"Can't she call him Oliver or Oscar?" suggested Jane.

"I'm afraid if I suggest a new name, she might change the animal on me. And we already started researching otters, which are really sort of cute."

"Maybe you could change his name later," said Alice. "Sometimes people do that when they have babies at the hospital. One day they're calling the baby Hortense after someone's great-grandmother, and the next day they've changed it to Hannah."

"That's not a bad idea, Aunt Alice," said Cynthia. "I could wait until the proof stage to suggest it."

"What's your story about?" asked Ethel.

Cynthia rolled her eyes. "Good question. The book is supposed to have to do with conservation, from an animal's perspective. At least that's where we are

right now. I can't believe it's taken us nearly a week to get that far."

"That sounds like it has potential," said Alice hopefully.

"Maybe," said Cynthia. "Mind if I take some of these gingersnaps along with our morning tea?"

"Not at all," said Jane.

Jane fixed an appealing tea tray, complete with a little bouquet of flowers just delivered from Wild Things, and sent Cynthia back to her challenging task.

"Good luck with Bucky Otter," called Jane.

They heard Cynthia groan as she went through the swinging door.

"Poor Cynthia," said Alice.

"That's right," said Jane, "and the next time I start feeling sorry for myself for having to cook for that woman, I need to remember that at least I don't have to spend the whole day working on a book with her."

"Whatever they're paying Cynthia is probably not nearly enough."

"I still don't know what's wrong with Bucky Beaver," said Ethel.

Chapter ❄ Eighteen

"What are you going to dress up as?" Jane asked Alice, as the two of them were finishing some of the party preparations Friday afternoon.

"Dress up?" repeated Alice as she put the large mixing bowl away.

"You know, for the party. Everyone is supposed to come as a favorite character from a musical."

"Oh, I guess I forgot. I can't even think of a musical offhand."

"Well, just remember back to when you were a kid and some musical that you really loved."

"The only one that comes to mind is *The Wizard of Oz*."

"No!" said Jane as she closed the dishwasher. "You can't do that one."

Alice laughed. "I wasn't planning on it. It's just the only one I can think of at the moment."

"Sorry." Jane smiled. "It's just that I want to come as Dorothy. I already have the outfit. I did it once at the restaurant for Halloween. I even have these great ruby slippers."

"Oh, you'll be a perfect Dorothy," said Alice.

Jane studied Alice. "You could be another character from *The Wizard of Oz*."

"Which one?"

"How about Glinda?" offered Jane. "She was fair like you and very lovely."

Alice laughed. "Somehow I just don't see myself in a sparkling gown."

Jane considered this. "Well, how about the Scarecrow then?"

"The Scarecrow?" Alice nodded. "That wouldn't be too bad."

"I could lend you my overalls."

Alice waved her hand. "They would never fit."

"Don't be so sure, they're big on me."

"Well, we could try. After all, the scarecrow was supposed to be stuffed with straw, so maybe I can stuff myself into your overalls."

"We're all done in here for now," said Jane. "Want to traipse over to Sylvia's and see if we can find anything to inspire us?"

"Let's," said Alice, "I've been dying to put on my boots and try out that snow."

The two sisters acted like schoolgirls as they threw snowballs and laughed and joked on their way to town. Stopping at the Coffee Shop for hot cocoa, they were immediately questioned by Hope and several others about the upcoming protest.

"Is it really true that Victoria Martin is going to be at the racetrack?" asked Betsy Long.

"I already told her that's what your aunt told me just this morning," said Hope, teasing her friend, "but she just won't believe *me*."

"It's not that," said Betsy. "Ethel doesn't always get her facts straight."

Jane nodded. "She is a dear, but I'd have to agree with you."

"Hope is right on the money," said Alice. "Victoria Martin is planning to make an appearance."

"So, do you think we'll get to meet her if we go?" asked Betsy. "I mean that might give us some added incentive."

"We can't promise anything," said Alice. "Really, I think it's best that you come out of support for the cause. Those poor dogs need someone to defend them."

"Right," said Betsy. "I know that, but I just think it would be thrilling to meet Victoria Martin too. I always try to watch her show whenever I'm not working."

"Speaking of which," hinted Hope.

"Oh yeah, I better go," said Betsy as she glanced at the clock. "This was supposed to be a break. See you all on Saturday."

"I hope people aren't disappointed," said Jane in a quiet voice once the two of them were settled into a corner booth.

"In what?"

"In Victoria. I mean, she can be a little rude some-times."

"A bit abrupt," added Alice as she sipped her cocoa.

"It'll be sad if she hurts anyone's feelings."

"Well . . ." Alice sighed, "I guess we can't control that."

"Hey," called Carlene from the front of the coffee shop. "There you are."

They both looked up.

"You, Alice Howard," said Carlene as she came their way. "The woman of the hour."

"Oh, I don't know—"

"Don't act modest, Alice. What you did Wednesday was one of the bravest things I've ever witnessed . . . from a local anyway."

Alice shrugged. "I just did what I felt I should. Really, it wasn't much. To be perfectly honest, it was pretty embarrassing down at the jail."

"Mind if I join you girls?"

"Not at all," said Jane, scooting over to make room.

Carlene laid a large envelope on the table. "I just thought you might like to see these photos." She opened it up and slid out several black and white shots of Alice being surrounded by the angry racing fans.

"Oh my," said Alice, as she suddenly remembered how overwhelming it had really been.

"Wow!" said Jane. "I didn't realize that they'd really surrounded you like that." She pointed to a particularly angry man. "Look at that guy. It looks like he's about to hit you."

Alice felt a shudder go through her.

"These are good, Carlene," said Jane. "What are you going to do with them?"

"I wrote a story for our paper, but then I decided to make it available to the AP, and it's actually getting picked up by some papers around the state. Of course, I'm making mention of the next protest and how your friend Victoria Martin will be on hand to make a statement."

"Our friend?" Alice frowned. "I wouldn't go that far."

"Your guest, whatever. I don't think it really matters. The point is, people are paying attention. The event on Saturday promises to be a big deal." She grinned. "All because of you, Alice."

"Well . . ." Alice shrugged again.

"My sister is so modest," said Jane. "I'd probably be signing autographs for everyone."

"I won't take any more of your time," said Carlene,

standing. "I just thought you might like to know. Make sure you get a copy of the *Philadelphia Inquirer* tomorrow, Alice."

"Thanks, Carlene." Alice waved, then shook her head. "Goodness, it just keeps getting bigger."

"Does that make you uncomfortable?"

"Well, sort of, actually."

"Then just remember, it's for the dogs."

Alice brightened. "Yes, you're absolutely right, Jane. It's for the dogs."

"In fact, we could even say that we're going to the dogs." Alice grinned.

"Speaking of going, we'd better head over to Sylvia's now."

They spent a pleasant hour visiting with Sylvia and picking out a few things for Alice's scarecrow costume. Alice was content to let Jane take the lead in this since all things creative seemed to come under Jane's jurisdiction.

"Are you sure you have time for this?" she asked as they walked through the snow toward home. "I know you've got a lot on your plate right now, Jane."

"This will be simple really," Jane assured her. "Mostly just sewing on a few patches and making your burlap head cover-up. Unless you'd rather just wear makeup."

"I think it'd be fun to look as much like the original scarecrow as possible," said Alice.

"Good." Jane smiled. "I was hoping you'd get into the spirit of things."

"What's Louise going to dress as?" asked Alice.

"I'm not sure," said Jane, "but if she's willing, I'd love to talk her into being Glinda, the good witch. There are still some old prom dresses in the attic that could be worked into something suitable."

"Well, if anyone can talk Louise into this, it would be you."

"I don't know, Alice." Jane winked at her. "Lately, it seems like you've become the sister with the power of persuasion."

"How's that?"

"Well, look at what you've got going for everyone on Saturday."

Alice shook her head. It was ironic that she of all people should be the one to get something like this rolling. Really, who would have guessed?

Chapter ❄ Nineteen

After Jane and Alice returned to the inn that afternoon, they turned their attention to costumes for Saturday's party.

"I feel silly," complained Louise as Jane adjusted the inserts she had fashioned to make the old prom dress fit.

"You look lovely," said Alice. "That color suits you, Louise."

Jane had set up her sewing station in the kitchen so that she could keep an eye on her various baking projects for the party.

"I can't believe I agreed to do this," said Louise.

"You make a perfect Glinda," said Alice. "Even your hair is the right color."

"Was Glinda's hair silver?" asked Louise.

"Well," Alice said, "it was light."

"I have a blonde wig for you to wear," Jane mumbled through the pins in her mouth.

"I do not want to wear a wig," said Louise. "That is going too far."

"Why do *you* have a blonde wig, Jane?" asked Alice as she turned a page of the *Inquirer.*

Jane laughed. "Oh, I don't know. I was going through a phase."

"Hey, look at this," said Alice suddenly. She held up the newspaper so that they could see the black and white photo of her being mobbed by the angry racing fans. Louise adjusted her glasses and leaned forward to see.

"Oh my word!" she exclaimed.

"Wow," said Jane, "you really are a celebrity now."

"Not a very flattering photo," said Louise.

"Well, no."

"It's dramatic," said Jane as she returned to her pinning, "and that's what gets people's attention."

"I'm not sure I like this heading," said Alice. *"Animal Rights Activist Protests in Potterston.* I'm not really an animal rights activist. I don't belong to any organizations."

"Maybe they'll start recruiting you now," suggested Jane.

Then Alice read the article aloud to them. It was generally positive. "I wouldn't have minded if they'd left out my arrest," she said as she folded the paper and looked back at her sisters.

"That adds to the sympathy factor," said Jane as she placed the last pin and stepped back to admire her work. "You almost don't notice the inserts on the sides."

"I told you I would not fit into this old dress," said Louise.

"It wasn't that far off," Jane reminded her. "Not bad for, what, fifty years ago."

"Not quite." Louise stood straighter.

"What's going on in here?" said a familiar, but not necessarily welcome, voice. Alice turned in time to see Victoria coming through the swinging doors with Cynthia following her.

"We're doing a fitting," said Alice quickly. She stood up and attempted to send Cynthia a signal that this was not the best time to bring Victoria into the kitchen. She felt bad, since her job was to keep anyone from entering the kitchen during the fitting.

"Let's see," said Victoria, pushing past Alice.

Alice turned and saw her older sister's eyes flash with anger.

"Why in the world are you dressed like that, Louise?" demanded Victoria as if she had a right to know.

Louise scowled. "It is supposed to be my costume for the party tomorrow night. But I am not sure that I am—"

"Come on, Louise," pleaded Jane. "You said you'd do this." She turned to Victoria and Cynthia. "We wanted it to be a surprise, but we're doing *The Wizard of Oz*. I'm coming as Dorothy. Alice is the Scarecrow. And we want Louise to be Glinda."

"Which is perfectly ridiculous," said Louise.

"*Hmmm.*" Victoria nodded as she walked closer and seemed to study the dress. "You should put some glitter on the skirt," she suggested.

"Yes," said Jane, "that's my plan."

"*Oz?*" said Victoria with interest. "That's one of my favorite movies."

"What are you planning to dress as, Victoria?" asked Jane.

"I haven't had a chance to really consider it." Victoria shook her head. "It's a shame because I have some wonderful costumes at home, but none that are from musicals."

"I remember watching your Halloween show last year," said Jane. "You wore a pretty convincing witch costume."

Victoria nodded, then suddenly looked at Jane as if she had just struck gold. "That's it!" she exclaimed. "I could be the Wicked Witch of the West."

Jane grinned. "Oh, Victoria, that would be perfect. Would you like to join our cast for Oz?"

"Yes." Victoria nodded. "I'll call my assistant right this minute and have him ship the costume to me overnight."

"Now *I'm* feeling left out," said Cynthia sadly.

"Everyone has a part in Oz except me. Maybe I could dress up like Toto."

"No," said Jane. "I already have a little stuffed Toto to carry in my wicker basket."

"Well, there's still the Tin Man," said Victoria. "Although that might be difficult to pull off this late in the game."

"And the Cowardly Lion," offered Alice.

"You'd make a cute lion," said Jane. "I have some brown sweats that would probably work okay. I could make you a tail and trim the hood with yellow yarn like a lion's mane."

"Do you really have time for that, Aunt Jane?" asked Cynthia hopefully.

"I do as long as you all agree to one thing."

"What's that?" asked Cynthia.

"We all have to sing 'We're Off to See the Wizard' together."

Although her sisters protested that they would all go off-key if Jane sang, they finally agreed, and Victoria and Cynthia went back to work on their children's book.

"Cynthia said that the book is getting steadily worse," said Louise after the two went back to the library.

"Well, maybe delaying the deadline was a good idea after all," said Jane. "Now, turn around, Louise. I want to see if it's hanging straight."

Jane chuckled as her sister turned slowly around.

Louise frowned when she faced Jane. "Are you laughing at me?"

"No, no." Jane emphatically shook her head.

"Well, what then?" Louise looked unconvinced.

"Victoria," sputtered Jane. "Playing the Wicked Witch of the West. It's priceless!"

"I thought that would amuse you," said Alice.

"It *is* rather fitting," Louise said.

"Talk about typecasting," said Jane. "She won't even have to act to carry it off."

Later in the afternoon, Alice came up with an idea to help Jane. She decided to invite her ANGELs to serve at the party. "I thought they could dress up like Munchkins," said Alice.

"Oh, that'd be so adorable," said Jane, "and the extra help would be great."

Alice called up Ashley Moore and explained her idea, then asked her to call the others.

"Sure, Miss Howard," said Ashley eagerly. "I think that sounds like fun."

"Do the best you can with the costumes," Alice told her. "Do you even know what a Munchkin is?"

"Of course," said Ashley. "Everyone's seen *The Wizard of Oz*. We have the movie. I saw it, like, a zillion times when I was a little kid. I know all the songs by heart."

Alice smiled. "Good. Maybe you'll want to sing for us."

"Do you think we could sing the Munchkin song?" asked Ashley eagerly.

"I don't see why not. You talk to the other girls about it."

"Cool."

Alice was about to hang up when Ashley asked about the protest on Saturday.

"Yes, it's still on."

"Good, we're planning on coming. Hey, my mom showed me your article in the newspaper, Miss Howard. That was so cool."

Alice laughed. "Cool?"

"Yeah, it's like you're famous now."

After Alice hung up she wondered if this would be her fifteen minutes of fame. Not that she had ever wanted to be famous, but it was not so bad either.

Chapter ❄ Twenty

As Alice walked toward the stairway, she heard a sound coming from the hall. She turned to see Harold standing in the shadows with a package in his arms.

"Pssst," he said with his forefinger over his lips.

"What is it?" she whispered.

"Can you meet me in the parlor?"

She nodded, and then looked over her shoulder as if she was worried that someone was listening. Of course, she had no idea why she should care. Just the same, she tiptoed as she followed Harold into the parlor. Once in the parlor, he closed the door and set his package on a chair. "I need some help," he told her.

"Doing what?"

He sat down and began opening his package. "I wanted to keep this as a surprise until tomorrow night," he said. "I had Sylvia Songer help me with a costume, but she didn't have time to hem the pants. Do you know how to sew, Alice?"

She smiled. "I do."

He sighed in relief as he pulled out a pair of red and white striped pants and handed them to her.

"Wow," she said as she held up the satiny trousers. "These are bright."

He grinned. "I know. Wait until you see the whole outfit."

"So, who are you coming as?" She could see another garment in the bag that was royal blue. "Uncle Sam?"

"Close. *Yankee Doodle Dandy*. It's my favorite musical."

"It looks like Sylvia already pinned them up," said Alice as she examined the bottoms of the trousers. "This shouldn't take very long."

"Do you mind?" He looked hopeful. "I expect to pay you."

She waved her hand at him. "No, you don't need to do that." Then she got an idea. "Do you know how to sew at all, Harold?"

He shook his head. "I can't even thread a needle."

"Well, instead of just hemming these, I'm going to give you a little sewing lesson. How does that sound?"

He nodded. "That sounds great. I often wished that I'd had Lily give me a little instruction before she passed away, but she got so weak from her treatments."

"If you're going to be a bachelor, you should learn at least how to sew on a button and a few other tricks," Alice told him.

"I'd like that."

"Let me get my sewing basket."

"I'll be right here."

It was not long before Harold's Uncle Sam trousers were hemmed: one leg by Alice and the other by Harold. She even taught him how to sew on a button.

"Why, this is easy as pie," said Harold as he tied off the last knot.

"Have you ever made a pie?"

He grinned sheepishly. "Well, no. I'm even worse in the kitchen."

"What do you do for food when you're home?" she asked.

"Frozen dinners mostly."

She made a face and said, "I have another idea."

He smiled. "I think I like it already."

After a brief conversation with Jane, it was agreed that Harold would perform KP duty for dinner that night. This actually worked out well, since Alice was able to use the time to create more posters for the protest the next day. She just hoped it would not hurt the quality of the food—Jane was having a hard enough time with Victoria's negative commentary on her meals without actually having something wrong with the dinner.

"Everything okay in here?" asked Alice shortly before dinnertime.

"It's great," said Jane. "Harold is a natural."

"Oh, I don't know about that, but it is sort of fun. Plus, Jane lets me have samples. That in itself is a good incentive to work."

"Harold has practically made the cobbler single-handedly."

"I wouldn't say that." He laughed. "Of course, if it turns out well, I expect to take all the credit."

"And if it doesn't?" Jane pointed a wooden spoon at him with a threatening look in her eye.

He nodded. "I'll take the blame."

Jane laughed. "Glad we got that clear."

"Actually, you can blame anything you like on me," he offered, "although I don't know why you'd need to do that. As far as I'm concerned, your cooking is flawless."

"Well, thank you."

As Alice set the table in the dining room, she listened to the happy banter between Harold and Jane in the kitchen. Not for the first time, she sincerely thanked God for Grace Chapel Inn and the way it had ministered to the needs of the guests—as well as the sisters—over the past year. It was really quite amazing, beyond what any of them had hoped or dreamed.

"Is that dinner I smell?" asked Cynthia as she stuck her head into the dining room.

"It is." Alice smiled at her niece. "Are you done for the day?"

"I think so." Cynthia stepped in and looked around approvingly. "This room is always so pretty in the evening, with the candlelight, crystal and china. May I help with anything?"

"You can fill the water glasses," said Alice as she folded a napkin precisely.

Soon Cynthia returned with the water pitcher. "Victoria went to her room to freshen up," she said as she filled a glass. "I think she just needed a break from me. I know that I need one from her."

"Well, as you said, maybe it'll help to have her gone for a while tomorrow," said Alice. "It will give you some time to yourself."

Cynthia nodded. "I just wish I had something that was worthwhile to work on."

"How's Bucky Otter doing?"

Cynthia groaned. "He no longer exists. Now we have Rocky Robin."

"Well, at least that has something of a ring to it."

"I guess, but now I can't get Victoria off the early-bird-gets-the-worm theme."

"Oh."

"I'm already starting to imagine what it's going to feel like to go job hunting next week."

Alice patted Cynthia on the back. "Oh, don't give up yet."

She sighed. "It's hopeless, Aunt Alice. There is no way I am going to pull a book out of all the garbled notes that we've accumulated this past week. I could more easily pull a rabbit from my hat."

"Well, I'm praying for you both," said Alice. "I believe God is going to help you come up with something."

"Thanks, Aunt Alice. I really hope you're right."

Soon they were all seated around the dinner table. Tonight was Alice's turn to say grace.

"Dear Heavenly Father, we thank You for all Your gracious blessings on our lives, and we thank You for the food that's been so lovingly prepared by Jane and Harold. We ask that You bless it to our use. Amen."

"Amen."

Victoria looked slightly startled. "Did I hear you say that Harold helped to fix dinner?"

Alice smiled. "That's right. He was having a cooking lesson with Jane."

"A little bachelor home ec," said Jane. "And he did very well. I'd give him an A plus."

"He also had a little sewing lesson today," added Alice. "I'd give him an A plus in that too."

He winked at Victoria. "I think they're just trying to make me take care of myself so that they can send me on my way."

She smiled at him. "Oh, I don't see how that can be, Harold. It seems to me everyone is enjoying your company." She glanced over at Alice now. "Although, if it were I, I'd still want to keep you a helpless bachelor."

He frowned. "Why's that?"

"So you'll be more in need of a woman's abilities."

Alice wondered if Victoria was actually flirting

with Harold. However, Harold seemed to like it.

Finally it was time for Harold's creation. He went into the kitchen with Jane and emerged with a large peach cobbler that looked just as if Jane had made it. Of course, Alice knew from experience that Jane had probably stood over him each step of the way, making sure he was doing everything just right.

"Looks delicious," said Louise.

"You know what they say," said Harold as he began to serve it onto dessert plates. "The proof of the pudding is in the eating."

He put a generous dollop of whipped cream on each one, and Jane came out with coffee and tea.

"This is excellent," said Victoria. Suddenly the room got unexpectedly quiet. It was the first compliment she had given at any meal.

Jane stared at Victoria with a slight frown, but said nothing.

Louise nodded. "It is very good. Harold makes it nearly as well as Jane."

Jane gave Louise a half smile.

Before long the dessert plates were empty, and Alice was helping Jane to clear the table. Everyone else had retired to the parlor to listen to Louise play the piano. They had agreed to classical music tonight since they all knew that tomorrow night would be nothing but show tunes.

"That woman!" said Jane as she set a stack of dishes in the sink.

"Don't let her get to you," said Alice.

"How can I not?"

"Just remember that Victoria would feel threatened if she actually admitted that you were an excellent cook, Jane. You know that has to be it."

"I suppose you're right, but it's still irritating."

"I know."

"Just when I think I've got a handle on it and I'm not going to let that woman get under my skin, she gets me."

Alice laughed. "Maybe God is trying to teach you something."

"What?"

"That you must do what you do to please Him, not Victoria Martin."

"I know. I know."

Alice filled the kettle with fresh water and put it on the stove.

"So," said Jane. "Did you see Victoria flirting with Harold tonight?"

"Do you think she really was?"

"I do." Jane nodded. "How funny would that be?"

"He must be nearly twenty years older than she," said Alice as she turned on the flame.

"He's such a sweet old guy." Jane frowned. "In fact, I think he's way too good for someone like Victoria. Too bad Louise isn't attracted to him."

"I'm glad Louise didn't hear that."

"You're right. Please, don't tell her."

Chapter ❄ Twenty-One

Alice got up early on Saturday morning so that she could walk with Vera. Because of their hectic schedules, they had only walked once earlier in the week. She was surprised to see Victoria when she came down the stairs to the second floor.

"You're up early, Victoria."

"As you are." Victoria looked at her. "Do you jog like your sister Jane?"

Alice laughed. "No, but I do try to walk three times a week."

"Really?" said Victoria. "So do I. Unfortunately I haven't managed to do that this week." She patted her ample hips. "That and your sister's rich food are playing havoc with my figure."

As badly as Alice wanted to just slip out the door and hurry over to Vera's, she knew the proper thing to do would be to invite Victoria. "Would you like to join us?" she asked meekly.

"Us?"

"Yes, I walk with my friend Vera."

"Do you think Vera would mind if I came?"

"No, I'm sure she'd love to meet you."

"Well, just let me go and change my shoes," said Victoria.

Alice went downstairs to wait. She considered calling Vera to warn her, but did not want to risk being overheard by Victoria.

"All ready," said Victoria as she came down the stairs in a fancy pair of athletic shoes.

It was cold and crisp outside, but the snow from Thursday was nearly gone.

"I hope we get snow again soon," said Alice.

Victoria looked up at the clear morning sky. "Well, fortunately, I don't think that's going to happen today. I would not enjoy protesting at the dog races during a blizzard."

"No, I don't think I would either."

"Now, who is this friend Vera?"

"She teaches fifth grade," said Alice. "Her husband Fred runs the local hardware store."

"Must be nice," said Victoria.

"To run a hardware store? Or teach?" Alice felt confused.

"Neither," said Victoria. "Well, and both, I mean it must be nice to live such an ordinary life."

"Oh." Alice wondered how Vera would feel about that kind of description of her life.

"Sometimes I wonder what my life would be like if I hadn't become so well known and successful. Now I can hardly go anywhere or do anything without everyone knowing me by name. It's really a hardship, you know."

"I really wouldn't know," said Alice. "Although some of my ANGELs feel certain that I must be a celebrity now that I've had my picture in the *Inquirer*."

Victoria made a noise that sounded similar to laughter. "Oh, there are plenty of benefits to my life," continued Victoria. "All my homes and my travels and being treated with respect wherever I go, but still . . . sometimes one wonders."

"This is Vera's house," said Alice, waving at Vera in her kitchen window.

Alice introduced the two women, quickly explaining to Vera that Victoria had decided at the last minute to join them. "I assured her you wouldn't mind," she said.

"Not at all," said Vera with a cheerful smile. "Not everyone can say they've walked with Victoria Martin."

Victoria sniffed. "Yes, I was just saying to Alice how fortunate you both are to be able to live such simple lives."

Vera's brows lifted slightly. "Simple?" she repeated.

Victoria waved a cashmere-gloved hand at her. "Oh, it's not a bad thing. I mean that you get to go about your daily tasks and chores without constantly being recognized by the public."

"Oh." Vera nodded as if she understood, but Alice suspected she was only being polite. It was fortunate that she and Vera had both decided to do only a short walk. Thirty minutes would be more than enough time if the conversation continued like this.

"Are we walking too fast for you?" asked Vera.

"No, not at all. I actually go much faster than this when I'm with Rob and Roy."

"Rob and Roy?" echoed Vera.

"Oh, those are my dogs," said Victoria. "My babies."

"I see."

"A pair of beautiful Doberman pinschers," said Victoria. "Oh, how I miss the boys."

"Victoria is going to the protest with us today," said Alice.

"So I've heard," said Vera. "Should be quite an event."

"Yes," agreed Victoria. "Certainly, it will be much better attended than poor Alice's last effort."

"Well, at least Alice got the wheels rolling," said Vera generously. "I would've gone myself, but we had, uh, other pressing matters to attend to at my school."

"That's right," said Victoria. "Alice says you are a teacher. How nice."

"I'm not sure that I'd call it nice," said Vera, "but I do find it fulfilling. I must say I love the children."

"I'm writing a children's book," said Victoria.

"Really?" said Vera with interest, although Alice knew good and well that this was old news to Vera. "How's it coming?"

Victoria frowned. "Not too well, I'm afraid. My editor and I just can't seem to see eye-to-eye."

"Have you written other books for children?" asked Vera.

"Well, no, but I have written cookbooks and decorating books and even one on gardening."

"Do you know much about children?" asked Vera.

"As much as anyone, I suppose."

Vera nodded. "Do you have children or grandchildren?"

"Oh no." Victoria shook her head. "I never had time for that."

"I see."

"I don't think that matters so much. My publisher has full confidence in my ability to carry this off."

"Right." Vera looked amused now. "Have you read many children's books?"

"Well, no. There's been no reason to."

"Maybe it would help if you read some," suggested Vera.

"You know, that's not a bad idea," said Victoria. "I wonder where I could get some."

"I have quite a few picture books still," said Vera. "They're too young for my fifth graders, but I'm saving them for my grandchildren."

"You have grandchildren?" asked Victoria.

"Not yet. But I have two grown daughters and I expect it's only a matter of time. Although I'm in no hurry."

"Perhaps you could pick out some of the better books and lend them to me," said Victoria.

"Sure." Vera wore an expression that Alice could not read, but she seemed perplexed about something.

"How's Fred?" asked Alice.

"Okay," said Vera. "Although he's worried that the new snow shovels haven't arrived yet. He's sure that we're going to have the big snow any day now, and every year he gets at least a dozen people coming in to replace their snow shovels." Vera chuckled. "Now, if they weren't such tightwads and bought the sturdy metal ones in the first place, they wouldn't have to replace them so often. But then those plastic ones are temptingly cheap."

"Why does your husband carry cheap plastic snow shovels?" asked Victoria.

"Because that's what some people want," said Vera. "Of course, he always has the good ones too."

The threesome got quiet as they did the return loop back toward Vera's house. Vera seemed to be concentrating hard on something.

"Do you and Fred have your costumes for tonight?" asked Alice as Vera's house came within sight.

"We do," said Vera. "I'm coming as Molly Brown and Fred is coming—now don't laugh—as Moses."

"Moses?" said Victoria. "*The Ten Commandments* was not a musical."

"I know." Vera shook her head. "I've tried and tried to tell him, but he just won't listen. The truth is Fred hates musicals."

"But why Moses?" asked Alice.

"*The Ten Commandments* is his favorite movie," said Vera as they reached her front yard. "Besides, it was easy. He's just wearing his bathrobe over his clothes with a stick-on beard." Her brow furrowed slightly as she glanced up at her house and that was when Alice knew exactly what was bothering her good friend. Vera was a busy full-time schoolteacher and was not overly fond of domesticities. She was probably not eager to have Victoria Martin walking through her house and seeing how "ordinary" people

172

lived. Alice knew for a fact that what little cleaning was done at the Humberts was usually done on Saturdays.

"Why don't you go through your picture books and drop them by the inn later today," suggested Alice.

"That's a good idea," said Vera, looking considerably relieved. "I'll do that on my way to the protest rally. Did I tell you that several of my fifth graders asked to go with me? I think it's important that they're taking an interest in something like this."

"Well," said Victoria, pausing as if to catch her breath. "What kind of children don't love and care about dogs?"

"That's true," said Vera.

"See you later," said Alice.

"Nice meeting you," called Victoria as they turned around and began heading back to the inn.

"Are you getting winded?" asked Alice, slowing down a bit. She would feel horrible if Victoria Martin keeled over from a heart attack.

"I'm all right." Victoria said, huffing slightly.

Alice slowed it down a bit more.

"Your friend seems nice," said Victoria. "Although I don't know how she can stand the color of her house. I think it is absolutely hideous."

Alice had never been crazy about the mustard yellow, but she would never dream of mentioning this to Vera. "The color is a common one for old homes in this part of the country. But it wasn't something Vera chose. Fred used that paint because of a mix-up at the hardware store a few years back. Apparently a customer had ordered the wrong paint number and when he saw the color, he was very upset and wanted something else."

"*Oops.*"

"Fred had already mixed about twenty gallons of it. The original color was a bright canary yellow, but Fred managed to tone it down to a more traditional shade."

"It was the customer's mistake," said Victoria as they reached the walk. "He should've made him pay for it."

"Fred's not like that."

"Amazing that man can stay in business."

"He put the paint on sale, but by the end of the summer it was still sitting there. Fred knew his own house needed painting, so finally he just decided to use it himself."

"Good grief," said Victoria. "I wouldn't paint my house that color if someone offered me millions to do it."

By now they were at the front door, and Alice was greatly relieved. "Excuse me," she told Victoria. "I'm going to run up and take a shower now."

"See you at breakfast," said Victoria as she flopped herself down on the bench in the foyer.

"I hope we didn't wear you out," called Alice.

"Not," she gave a little gasp, "at all."

Chapter ❄ Twenty-Two

When Alice came to breakfast, only Jane and Louise were still there. "Where's everyone?" she asked as she sat down and poured herself a cup of tea.

"Harold went to town for something," said Louise, "and Victoria went to her room looking somewhat fatigued."

"Oh dear," said Alice. "She walked with Vera and me, and I'm afraid we went too fast. I hope she's okay."

"I'm sure she's fine. Cynthia didn't even seem to mind. She's getting caught up on her e-mail."

"Quiche?" offered Jane as she handed the pie plate to Alice. "I figured we'd better fortify ourselves this morning," said Jane. "It's going to be a long day."

"It's cold out there," said Alice. "Don't forget to put on your long johns."

"Hey, that's not a bad idea," said Jane.

"I don't own long johns," said Louise.

"I've got some you can borrow," offered Alice.

Louise poured herself another cup of coffee and sighed. "I'll be glad when things settle down and we can get back to an ordinary routine."

"What is ordinary?" asked Jane.

"According to Victoria, we are," said Alice.

"*Yoo-hoo,*" called Ethel from the kitchen, "anyone home?"

"In the dining room," called Jane.

"Oh, I thought you'd be done with breakfast by now."

"We're just enjoying a bit of leisure while we can," said Jane. "Make yourself at home."

"Thank you." Ethel removed her jacket, poured herself a cup of coffee and sat down next to Alice. "I thought you'd all be glad to know that everything is just fine between Lloyd and me."

"That's good," said Alice.

"So, Lloyd's not going to be coming around here and challenging Harold to a duel or anything?" teased Jane.

"No, of course not." Ethel chuckled. "Although Lloyd is not overly fond of our Harold. He wants to know exactly how long he plans to stay."

"I was wondering that myself," said Louise.

"Oh, he's just lonely," said Jane.

"Even so, I'm sure he's not planning on taking up residency in the inn," said Ethel.

"Well, he at least has to stay until our little party," said Jane. "After all, he's our main entertainment."

"I suppose," said Ethel. "I'll just have to make sure to keep him and Lloyd safely apart tonight."

"Really, Auntie," said Jane. "I can't imagine that Lloyd would have any hard feelings toward our sweet Harold."

Ethel patted her hair. "Lloyd Tynan, it seems, is a very possessive man when it comes to me."

"So how's his bowling coming?"

"Oh, I think he may be getting bored with it. He told me that he really dislikes coming home smelling like an ash tray every bowling night. It seems there is a bar right next to their lanes and the smoke drifts over."

"Sounds lovely," said Louise.

"So, I'm hoping he'll give it up before long."

"Did you get your costume yet?" asked Jane.

Ethel smiled. "Actually, I'm still working on both our costumes."

"Both?"

"Lloyd and I are coming together."

"As what?" asked Louise.

"Oh, I can't tell," said Ethel coyly. "It's supposed to be a surprise."

"Speaking of Lloyd," began Alice, "did he make up his mind yet?"

"His mind?"

"About coming to the protest today."

"Oh, that." Ethel made a face. "Now, it's not that I don't like dogs, because I do, in their place, which isn't in my house. But, growing up on a farm and then marrying a farmer, well, I just don't go in for all this animal-rights business. The next thing you know we'll all be eating soy burgers and wearing pleather." She grinned. "I read that in one of my magazines."

"This isn't exactly about animal rights," said Alice. "It's more about preventing the cruel and inhumane treatment of racing dogs. You should see some of the photos that Jane's found on the Internet."

"Yes," said Jane. "It's really appalling."

"Be that as it may, Lloyd and I have both decided it's for the best to avoid the protest today. I told him that I would tell you and that you'd all understand. You do, don't you?"

"Well," said Alice as she picked up her plate, "I think if you knew more about this, you'd—"

"You have to look at my photos, Aunt Ethel," said Jane as she got up.

Even from the kitchen, Alice could hear her aunt still talking to Louise. "It's not that I don't care," she told her. "It's just that I think all these claims of dog abuse are a little overblown."

"Oh, but I don't think—"

"We all know that Alice is a very sensitive person," said Ethel. "She can barely even kill a spider. I've seen her trap one in a mason jar and then let it loose in the garden. We can't all be like that."

Louise said something in response, but Alice could not hear her as she turned on the sink faucet and began rinsing plates and loading them into the dishwasher. It was odd, thought Alice, that her own aunt was taking an opposing position, but someone like Victoria Martin was supportive. Then, Ethel often held opinions that differed from Alice and her sisters. *No need to obsess over it,* she told herself as she closed the door to the dishwasher.

"Oh my word!" said Ethel, loud enough to be heard over the water running in the sink.

Alice turned off the faucet, dried her hands and hurried out to the dining room to see what the problem was. Without saying anything, she simply stood in the doorway and watched. Jane had spread her posters with the blown-up photos from the Internet across the dining room table in a most dramatic fashion.

"Oh dear!" Ethel looked horrified, her hand clasped over her mouth, as she looked from poster to poster of suffering and deceased greyhound dogs.

"Goodness," said Louise sadly. "They look even more pitiful when the photos are enlarged."

Ethel shook her head. *"Tsk-tsk.* I had no idea."

"See," said Jane, pointing her finger with conviction. "It's a lot more serious than most people assume."

"I can see I was wrong," said Ethel.

Alice slipped back into the kitchen to finish cleaning up. She knew there was no need for her to say anything. The photos were shocking, even to Alice, who had seen most of them before.

Finally Ethel came into the kitchen and patted Alice on the back. "Don't you worry, dear," she told her. "I'm going to go call Lloyd the minute I get home. I expect we'll both be there today."

"Thanks," said Alice with a grateful smile.

"I really didn't believe it was that bad."

"Most people don't."

"I want to bring Lloyd over here to see Jane's photos too."

Alice nodded as she wiped down the kitchen table.

"If he feels as passionate about this as I do now, he may even want to say a few words at the rally today. Would that be okay, Alice?"

"Of course. I was hoping he would."

"Oh good." Ethel clapped her hands. "What a day this is going to be."

Chapter ❄ Twenty-Three

"Whom shall I ride with today?" asked Victoria as they were preparing to leave for the protest.

"Oh right," said Louise, "Cynthia is staying home to work. Well, you are certainly welcome to ride with Jane and me. We do not plan to stay as long as Alice, so we are taking separate cars."

"Or you could ride with me," Alice offered, although she seriously doubted that Victoria Martin would want to ride in her little Toyota.

"Perhaps you would rather take the Mercedes and simply follow us," suggested Jane. "If you would be more comfortable."

Victoria looked slightly surprised. "Oh, I don't drive."

"Really? How do you get around?" asked Louise.

Victoria smiled, perhaps a bit smugly. "Oh, I have drivers, of course."

"Of course," said Jane as she filled a thermos with coffee.

"I'm ready," said Alice as she slipped on her warmest gloves. "I'll go ahead since I have the signs."

"I think I'll go with Alice," announced Victoria.

Alice nodded. "I apologize for my humble wheels. My car isn't fancy, Victoria."

Victoria waved her hand dismissively. "As long as

it's mechanically sound and won't run out of gas, I promise not to complain."

Jane winked at Alice.

"Well, I think I can guarantee that much." Alice opened the front door.

"I do believe it's gotten colder out," said Victoria as they stepped out to the porch.

"I'm glad the heater works well," said Alice as they walked over to where her car was parked. "I hope you're dressed warmly, Victoria."

"I'm wearing my silk long underwear," she said, "as well as a lot of layers."

"Good for you."

"This isn't so bad," said Victoria as she surveyed the interior of Alice's car. "I'm sure it's very economical for you."

Alice nodded and started the ignition. "And dependable."

Soon they were on their way, with Alice praying a silent prayer for the day ahead. She only partially listened as Victoria rambled about how many cars she owned.

"Of course, there's the Land Rover in New Hampshire." She laughed. "And I nearly forgot about the Jaguar in Malibu. It's a convertible."

"That's a lot of vehicles for someone who doesn't even drive," commented Alice.

"Isn't it. But just because I don't drive doesn't mean I don't need to get around. Normally I like to get around in style."

Once again, Alice felt like apologizing for her car, but she did not.

"I think the media people plan to start showing up around one," said Victoria. "That's what my publicist told me.

Alice nodded. "Do you think there will be a lot?" She did not want this to turn into some crazy circus event.

"It's hard to say. It depends on what else is going on in the area. So far I haven't heard of anything too sensational—no bombings, plane crashes or violent crimes."

"Thank goodness," said Alice.

"I'd considered asking my assistant to drive down and bring Rob and Roy. I thought it would be awfully clever to have my dogs protesting the abuse of dogs. Don't you think?"

"I'm sure the media people would've liked that, but would your dogs have liked the crowds and noise?"

"Probably not. They're very protective of me and don't always know exactly who is friend or foe. I'm sure they're better off at home."

"Have you always had dogs?"

"Not always. There was a period of about ten or fifteen years, back when I was getting my career off the ground when I had neither the time nor energy for pets. Nor family or children either for that matter. Probably one of the reasons I've never married." She turned to peer at Alice. "Have you ever been married?"

"No. I had a romance in college that had promise, but it didn't work out."

"Oh yes," said Victoria quickly. "The same thing happened to me."

"Really?" Alice waited to see if Victoria wanted to say more.

"Yes. His name was George Harding. He was handsome, athletic, intelligent. Oh my, he was really something." Victoria leaned back and sighed.

"What happened?"

"I don't usually tell people this, but you seem like a trustworthy person, Alice," said Victoria.

"Your secrets are safe with me," Alice assured her.

"Well, I was only nineteen at the time, but, believe me, I was completely smitten by this man. I could see myself cooking and cleaning for him, doing his laundry and darning his socks. I imagined us living in a little cottage with pale blue shutters and a white picket fence, maybe by the sea. I would grow beautiful roses and we would have had lots of children. I imagined perhaps four or five. Oh yes, and a cat and a dog too. It was going to be a perfect life."

"And?"

Victoria sighed. "Oh, George enjoyed my company for about a year. Then Margaret Spencer came along."

"Margaret Spencer?"

"Only the most gorgeous woman in the college. She took campus by storm as a freshman. Oh my, she had a thick mane of blonde curls, long legs, sparkling blue eyes and a smile that was truly captivating. All the boys were just crazy for Maggie Spencer."

"And did George fall for her too?"

"Not only did he fall for her, but he married her as soon as he graduated. They were the toast of the campus that year. Their pictures are on every other page of the yearbook."

"Oh."

"Yes." Victoria shook her head. "I was heartbroken. Devastated. The remainder of my college experience passed by in a bit of a foggy blur. I actually started drinking quite heavily during my junior year. How I ever managed to graduate with a home economics degree is still something of a mystery to me, but I do have the certificate to prove it. It hangs on the wall in my office."

Alice chuckled. "Look at you now, Victoria, and what you have made of your life. It's really quite spectacular, don't you think?"

"I suppose."

Alice felt sorry for Victoria. It seemed obvious that despite her multiple homes, expensive cars, and highly visible, profitable career, this woman was not happy.

"I know I'm not like you, Victoria," began Alice, "but I have found a certain satisfaction in my unmarried life."

"Really?" Victoria sounded skeptical.

"Yes. I like knowing that I can pretty much come and go as I please. Of course, I check in with my sisters now that they live at home, but I've always enjoyed the simplicity of making my own choices. I can spend my time doing what I like, even if that means doing nothing at all. I like being able to read in bed until midnight, or making peanut butter on toast for breakfast. You know, little things like that."

"I suppose."

"And even though my college sweetheart is still sort of in the picture—"

"What?" said Victoria. "Don't tell me you're still dating the man you loved in college?"

"Well, not exactly." Alice smiled. "We hadn't seen each other in nearly forty years, and then last fall he unexpectedly popped back into my life."

"*Really?*"

"Yes. I was shocked at first, but then we spent some time together, getting reacquainted and filling in the blank spaces. It was actually nice. I discovered that we'd both grown and changed over the years."

"But hadn't he married?"

"To my surprise, he hadn't. His career is very demanding, and apparently he just never had the time or the inclination."

"How remarkable. So, do you think that you'll get married?"

"Well, the subject did come up. To be honest, I had mixed emotions about it. Then Mark was offered the opportunity of a lifetime. He's an exotic animal vet, you see, and he was invited to work with a research team in the Amazon."

"How extraordinary."

"Yes. That's where he is right now."

"Well, I never would've guessed that you would have such an exciting love life, Alice."

"Oh, I wouldn't go that far."

"I had fancies about a meeting with George a few years back . . ."

Alice waited.

"My alma mater was having a forty-year reunion for the decade of the 1960s. That's when George and I both attended. Well, I knew there was a good chance that George wouldn't be there, but I'd seen a show on television about people who met their lost loves at reunions . . ." She laughed. "I thought, well, maybe that was going to happen to me."

"I've heard stories like that too," admitted Alice.

"So, I spent about eight months dieting, faithfully working out with my personal trainer, and I even got some rather minor plastic surgery done." She glanced quickly at Alice. "I'm trusting you not to repeat this."

Alice nodded. "You can trust me, Victoria."

"Yes, I believe I can. So, I had my hair done just right and basically looked better than I'd looked in years, possibly even better than in college, although the years do have a way of catching up with us. But for my age, I was looking good. In fact, I still watch tapes of my television shows during that time just to remind myself of how good I can look when I really put my mind to it."

"And how did it go?"

"Well, I got to campus with my usual entourage.

Naturally, there were some local media people there doing spots on the returning college graduates who'd been successful."

Alice could just imagine a sleek and perfectly coifed Victoria emerging from an expensive limo with cameras flashing.

"It was really fun. I had people I couldn't even remember coming up to me and saying how much they'd liked me back in our college days." She laughed sadly. "Naturally, I hadn't the slightest clue who they were. But finally, just before dinner, I managed to ask someone about George Harding. I did it in a very nonchalant manner, as if I'd barely known him."

"You must've been nervous."

"A bit, but to be perfectly honest, I thought there was a pretty good chance that George would be bald and wrinkled with a potbelly that hung over his belt. That's how most of the other men were looking. Anyway, I was completely prepared to simply smile at him, say hello and just strut away. You know, show him just what he'd missed out on by not marrying me."

Alice chuckled. "So what happened?"

"It turned out he was there. My friend pointed him out across the room. And, as fate would have it, he still looked darn good. His hair was silver at the temples, but he was still handsome and athletic-looking. Standing next to him was his wife Maggie. No one had to tell me that it was she. And here is what seems completely unfair. That woman looked as if she'd barely aged at all. Still a gorgeous blonde with long legs and a smile that flashed clear across the room."

"Oh." Alice felt even more sorry for Victoria now. "Did you talk to George at all?"

"Just barely, but when Maggie discovered who I was, well, she would hardly leave my side. It seems she is one of my biggest fans. She regularly watches all my shows and has every one of my books. Not only that, but she assured me that she ran her household in exactly the way I prescribed."

"Didn't that make you feel good?" asked Alice. They were nearing the racetrack now and she wanted to bring this tale to a graceful ending.

"I suppose it should have, but all I could think of was how it should've been *me* taking care of George with such perfection. Here she was doing it, using my advice and know-how."

Alice put on her signal to turn toward the track. "That must have felt unfair."

Victoria nodded. "I'll say. It's like I'd been doing all the work, but Maggie was getting all the benefits."

Alice was parking her car now. Carlene had secured permission for them to park in a nearby parking lot of a business that was not open on Saturdays. "No need to take chances," she had advised Alice.

"That's quite a story, Victoria," said Alice as they climbed out of the car. She started unloading her signs.

"Here, let me help you with those," offered Victoria

in a slightly gruff voice. She took a small stack of signs under her arm.

"Thanks," said Alice as she closed the trunk.

"Now," said Victoria. "If you ever repeat that story, I'll have my attorneys all over you like freckles on an Irishman."

Alice started. "I would never."

Victoria nodded, then smiled. "I know. I was just checking."

Chapter ❄ Twenty-Four

Alice knew that today's protest was not about her, but she had to admit to herself that she felt a small twinge of dismay when Victoria captured all the limelight. It started with the few locals who had gathered along the street. As soon as they recognized Victoria Martin, they began to cluster around her, asking for autographs. Alice wondered if they had come here to protest or to get a glimpse of daytime television's domestic diva.

They had barcly taken care of the autographs and introductions, as well as a few photographs with local housewives posing next to the Queen of Cuisine, before the first media van came roaring down the street toward them.

"Where's the fire?" said Victoria dryly. The crowd around her all laughed.

"It's beginning," said Alice.

"Bring it on," said Victoria as she picked up a sign

and held it high. Others followed her example and within moments, the small crowd organized itself into an impressive protest group.

"Save the dogs!" a couple of teenagers began chanting as they marched up and down the street.

Soon, more protesters arrived, lining the streets with signs and enthusiasm, and more media vans began to show up. Alice spotted Louise and Jane walking toward them and thought that perhaps it was time to join her sisters. After all, Victoria seemed to have things under control with her fans and newscasters clamoring for her attention.

"Don't leave me," hissed Victoria into Alice's ear.

"Oh." Alice was surprised. "You want me to stay with you?"

"Yes." Victoria nodded vigorously. "I need someone I can count on by my side."

"Okay." Alice just waved to her sisters who had wisely brought folding chairs that they were now setting up farther on down the street.

"What is it that first drew your interest to this cause?" demanded a pretty brunette reporter as she shoved the microphone up close to Victoria's face.

"I've always been a dog lover," said Victoria just as cool and calm as you please. "I was appalled to learn of the inhumane treatment of greyhound racing dogs. I have friends in my home state who have founded a group that works to protect and adopt unwanted racing dogs."

"But what brought you to Potterston, Pennsylvania?" continued the woman. "Why have you suddenly become interested in this particular racing track?"

"I'm staying at a local inn," said Victoria. Now she winked at Alice. "It's located in the charming town of Acorn Hill."

"And how did you learn of the troubles over here in Potterston?"

Now Victoria put her arm around Alice's shoulder and pulled her into the shot. "My friend and innkeeper Alice Howard brought the issue to my attention when she first protested at this track just this week."

Now the microphone was thrust into Alice's face. "Are you the woman who was arrested after nearly being mobbed this week?"

"Oh, I wasn't—"

"That's right," said Victoria, pulling the microphone back to her. "Poor Alice was simply attempting to make a statement against the cruelty to dogs when racing patrons got angry and unruly."

"And then she was arrested?" said the woman.

"That's right. Naturally, she was released the same evening."

"What good do you think this protest will do?" asked another reporter.

"It will raise the level of public awareness," said Victoria. "When the good people of Potterston realize what kind of ugly business is going on at the racetrack, I'm sure they will want to do their part to help the poor dogs and maybe even get this place shut down."

"Do you really think the racetrack can be shut down?" asked the woman.

"Actually, I can't speak about the legalities of such things," said Victoria, "but I will say this." She paused to look intently at both of the cameras. "The senseless slaughter of young greyhounds, simply because their owners no longer consider them to be profitable, is a stain on our society."

So it went for the next hour. New media groups appeared and Victoria continued making her speeches. Alice recognized that Victoria was the perfect spokeswoman for this event. Even though Alice grew weary of the crowd's constantly pressing closer to get a peek at Victoria Martin, she never left her side and truly appreciated her participation.

Some of the racing fans jeered as they drove toward the track, but nothing got out of hand. Lloyd had taken on the role of unofficial event organizer, using his bullhorn to remind people that this was a peaceful rally and warning all protesters to stay clear of the street.

"There will be no blocking of traffic," he announced in a stern voice.

"Would you like some refreshments?" asked Jane after she had pushed her way through the small throng still clustered around Victoria. At that moment there were no camera interviews taking place, and Alice could tell that Victoria was getting weary.

"That would be lovely," said Victoria in a tired voice.

Then to Alice's surprise, Jane took Victoria by the arm and said, "Come with me." Jane pushed her way through the surprised onlookers and Alice followed.

"You two sit down," said Jane when they reached the section where Louise, Jane, and even Harold were comfortably arranged with chairs, picnic basket and, of course, their signs posted so all could see.

Soon Alice and Victoria were seated side by side. Jane put a red plaid blanket over their laps as Louise handed them each a steaming cup of cocoa.

"My, this is good," said Victoria after only one sip. "Do I taste a bit of cinnamon in here?"

Jane answered as she handed them sandwiches. "Yes, I find it gives an extra warmth to the cocoa."

Victoria nodded.

The sandwiches were simply egg salad, but made with, as always, the usual Jane flair. Alice was definitely enjoying hers.

"*Hmmm,*" said Victoria. "These are good. Do I detect a bit of nutmeg?"

Jane nodded, looking slightly stunned by this unexpected praise.

"I'll have to try that myself," said Victoria.

Alice smiled. After all the beautiful meals Jane had carefully prepared, this was the first compliment Victoria had ever given to Jane's culinary skills.

Across the street, the ANGELs were marching and singing the "Bingo" song now. They had started with "Who Let the Dogs Out?" Then they moved on to other dog tunes, like "How Much Is That Doggy in the Window?" Alice wondered just how many canine tunes they had in their repertoire.

"How are you two holding up?" asked Harold.

"Very well, thanks," said Victoria between bites.

"It looked as if you were in the midst of a media frenzy about ten minutes ago," said Louise as she sipped her coffee.

"It's impressive how much coverage we're getting," said Jane as she opened a tin of sugar cookies and offered them around.

"That's all thanks to Victoria," said Alice as she took a cookie.

Victoria waved her hand. "You can thank my publicist."

"Hello," called Ethel as she came over to join them. "My, this is quite an event, Alice. You can be proud."

Alice nodded to Victoria. "She's the main reason for the crowd."

"Well, they care about the dogs too, we hope," said Jane as she offered Ethel a cookie.

"Lloyd is doing a great job keeping the crowd in line," said Alice. "I'm glad you decided to come."

"Well, after seeing those photos," Ethel shook her head, "we couldn't not come."

"Lloyd wondered if this might be a good time to give a little speech," said Ethel. "Now that the news people are gone."

"I think that would be perfect," said Alice.

"By all means," agreed Victoria.

Lloyd got on his bullhorn again and called

everyone to attention. Then he gave an encouraging little pep talk. Ever the diplomat, he gave credit to Victoria, inviting her to stand as the crowd applauded. Then to everyone's surprise, Lloyd walked over and handed Victoria a giant brass key tied with a red ribbon. "Although we are in Potterston right now, on behalf of the citizens of Acorn Hill, we want to present you with this humble gift. It is the key to our town and the key to our hearts. We have all enjoyed your stay with us, and we hope that you'll come to visit us often."

"Well, thank you," said Victoria. "I'm honored. I have thoroughly enjoyed your charming little town as well as the hospitality at Grace Chapel Inn. Thank you, very much."

Another local media van came down the street. Victoria took a refill on the cocoa, and then she and Alice made it back to the corner where they had been standing. As before, Victoria gave an eloquent interview. As she was finishing, another van appeared, this one from one of the major network stations in Philadelphia.

The plan had been for the protest to last for about an hour or so, just long enough to make a real statement. It was getting ever colder, and some people had been there for a long time. The crowd slowly began to thin out. It was nearly two o'clock when the last media van, from another big station in Philadelphia, began packing up. Jane and Louise had gone home already, as had most of the citizens of Acorn Hill. Only a few stragglers remained, and it appeared that they were about ready to call it a day too.

"Should we go now?" asked Alice.

Victoria glanced around to see that only a couple of teenagers remained, probably from Potterston since Alice did not recognize them. "Yes. I think we've completed our business here."

Chapter ❄ Twenty-Five

As they were starting for Alice's car, a red pickup truck came speeding toward them from the direction of the racetrack. As the pickup turned onto the street, something fell from its bed, making a loud whack as it hit the ground.

"My goodness," said Victoria. "What on earth?"

"It's a dog crate," said Alice.

The truck continued down the road, despite the efforts of two boys who waved for the truck to stop.

Alice heard a yelping sound and began to run toward the crate. Soon she, Victoria, and the boys were kneeling next to it. "It sounds as if he's hurt," said Alice as the whimpering continued.

"Let's get him out of there," commanded Victoria.

Soon they had the box opened and Victoria was examining the buff-colored greyhound. "It looks like he's injured his hind leg," she said finally, stroking the dog's sleek coat. "He's cold," said Alice, removing her coat to cover him.

"Let's get him into the car."

"Want some help?" offered one of the boys.

"Thanks," said Alice. "It's just over here."

The taller boy easily lifted the lightweight dog and carried him over to her car, waiting while she opened the door and spread a blanket on the back seat. Then the boy gently slid in the dog. The other boy had gathered up what remained of the protest signs and carried them over to her car. "Thanks," said Alice as she opened the trunk and he put them in. "Thanks to both of you."

"No problem," said the taller one. "This is, like, a real rescue."

Alice nodded. "We better see about getting this dog to the vet," she told them.

"Good luck," called the shorter boy.

Victoria had gotten into the backseat with the injured dog. "Poor thing," she was saying in a soothing voice.

"Everything okay back there?" asked Alice as she leaned over to peer inside.

"Here's your coat back," said Victoria as she wrapped the still shivering dog in the blanket. He yelped in pain as she tucked it around him. "It's okay, boy," she said soothingly, and then asked Alice, "Do you know where the closest vet is?"

"I think I do," said Alice. "I just hope he's open."

"I've got my cell phone," said Victoria. She reached for her purse and began digging around to find it. "Here." She handed it to Alice. "Why don't you call?"

Alice frowned. "I don't know how to use one of those things."

Victoria laughed and took the cell phone back. First she got information and then she handed the phone to Alice. "I don't know the name of the clinic."

Alice asked for the phone number and waited until she was connected. Fortunately, the vet was in and Alice quickly explained their situation and said they would be right over. She handed the phone back to Victoria and, closing the back door, went around to the driver's side. That is when she saw the red pickup just pulling up beside her.

"Hey, have you seen my dog, lady?" demanded a man who appeared to be in his thirties. He had on a black leather jacket and an angry expression. Then he peered in the window and spotted Victoria and the dog in the backseat.

"The dog crate fell off your truck." Alice told him.

"I know." The man scowled. "I noticed that when I got to the gas station."

Now Victoria got out of the car. "What's the problem?" she asked.

"This is the owner of the dog," said Alice.

"Well, did you know that your dog is injured?" countered Victoria.

"Oh, he's probably just fine." The man leaned over and looked in the car. "Come on, Zipper, let's go now."

The dog let out a painful yelp.

"See," said Victoria. "He needs to be treated."

"Well, that's my business," snapped the man. "Gimme my dog."

"Not so fast," said Victoria, stepping in front of the man. "First I need to ask you whether you intend to have him treated or not."

"Look, lady, this dog is my property. I own him and can do whatever I see fit to him."

"Not according to the law."

"Outta my way, lady."

"Not until I know exactly what you plan to do with him," said Victoria without batting an eyelash.

Just then another pickup truck pulled up. "What's the problem, Jack?" called the man from the other truck.

"These old broads have kidnapped my dog," yelled Jack.

"That's not true," said Alice. "The dog was injured when his crate fell off the truck. We were about to get him some medical attention."

"He's my dog," said Jack. "I'll be the one to see to his needs."

Victoria stood up even straighter now, looking Jack directly in the eyes. "The dog's been injured. He is most likely lame. Tell me the truth, Jack, what do you really intend to do with him?"

"Listen, lady, he's my dog and my business, and even if I do plan to put him down, it's got nothing to do with you and your tree-hugging, animal-loving, fanatical friends. So just mind your own business."

Alice had noticed the other man in the pickup using his cell phone. Now she saw a pair of patrol cars slowly turning off the highway and coming down the road that led to the track.

"Look, Jack," said Victoria, not backing down for a minute. "How much would you like for your dog? I can afford to pay good money."

He looked tempted for a moment but then suddenly changed his mind. "He's not for sale, lady."

"Why not?" she pleaded. "He's of no use to you once he's lame."

"It's the principle."

"But you're only going to kill him," she said. "Why not let me take him and find him a good home?"

"Because I said *no*." He made a fist. "Give me back my dog."

"I will not," said Victoria. She climbed into the car. "Let's go, Alice."

Alice followed Victoria's orders and got inside. "Victoria," she said. "The police are coming. This could get messy."

"I am not going to give this poor dog back to that animal," she seethed. "He will only kill it. Maybe even brutally now that I've made him mad."

"But what about the police?"

"They will understand."

Alice opened her door and got out of the car as the officer approached.

"Mind if I ask you ladies some questions?" said the policeman.

Alice nodded, as did Victoria who remained in the back seat.

"Hey, aren't you the woman we arrested a few days ago?" asked the officer. "Hey, Sarge," he called over

200

his shoulder. "You better get over here and see this."

Alice now saw Sergeant Crane coming their way. She wished that the parking lot would open and swallow her up. "Hello," she said weakly.

"What's going on today, Miss Howard?" he asked with what seemed like genuine interest.

"Well," she began. Then slowly, searching for the right words, she told him about their dog rescue, assuring him that they most certainly were not dognappers.

"But then I came back," said Jack. "And now they won't give me my dog."

"Is that true?" asked Sergeant Crane.

"My friend wants to buy the dog," said Alice.

"The dog is *not* for sale!" yelled Jack.

"Settle down," said Sergeant Crane.

"The dog is injured and we know that it's common practice to kill dogs that can no longer run."

"It's none of your business," said Jack.

"It's wrong," said Alice. "Please, why can't you just sell us the dog? As my friend says, she can well afford it. You just name the price."

Jack was looking tempted, but his friend gave him an elbow and a dark scowl. "You gonna let these females tell you how to live your life?" demanded his friend.

"That's right," said Jack. "The dog's not for sale. I want him back."

Sergeant Crane looked at Alice. "Sounds like the dog's not for sale."

Alice felt seriously close to tears. "But why not?" she pleaded with Jack. "You know that you don't really want him."

Jack folded his arms across his chest and just looked away.

"I'm sorry," said Sergeant Crane. "Your friend is going to have turn over that dog."

Alice leaned over and motioned through the window to Victoria to come out. Victoria just sat there shaking her head. Then Alice started to open the door, but discovered it was locked. Of course, her keys were inside, already in the ignition. "Victoria!" she called, tapping on the window. "Unlock the doors."

Again, Victoria just shook her head and continued petting the dog.

"Oh dear." Alice looked up at Sergeant Crane. "I don't know what to do."

"May I have your permission to enter your car, Miss Howard?" asked Sergeant Crane.

Alice frowned. "Are you going to break a window?"

"No." He laughed. "We have easier ways."

"Okay."

"I'll be right back," he told her.

Now Alice pounded even harder on the window. "Please, Victoria," she yelled. "You've got to let him take his dog. Open the door."

Victoria was totally ignoring her. Despite Alice's pity for the dog, she was getting irritated at Victoria. What possible good did she think this was going to do?

Soon, Sergeant Crane returned with a long flat metal strip that he used to unlock Alice's car. Then he leaned in to speak to Victoria. "Do you want to hand over that dog, ma'am? Or do I need to take you in?"

"I refuse to surrender this poor animal to an owner who will most likely kill him before the night is over." She narrowed her eyes. "There are laws protecting animals, you know."

The sergeant scratched his head. "That's true enough, but you are breaking the law by not returning this man's dog to him."

"That's right," said Victoria. "I have offered to pay him for the dog, and to take the dog in for medical attention."

"I know. I know." Sergeant Crane stood up and motioned to the other officer. "I need some backup here."

Soon the two policemen had managed to extract a very stubborn Victoria Martin from the backseat of Alice's car. Alice was thankful the media were not around to get this. It would have surely made the news across the country.

The younger officer put her in handcuffs, recited her rights to her and then led her off to one of the patrol cars.

"I'll meet you at the station," called Alice, hoping that she was not about to be arrested too, perhaps as an accomplice.

"Now," said Sergeant Crane turning his attention back on Alice. "As for you. How do you keep managing to get yourself into these situations?"

"We were simply having a peaceful protest," Alice told him. "If the crate hadn't fallen from the—"

"Yes, yes." Sergeant Crane frowned. "Well, the truth is, I'm an animal lover myself. Your friend is right. Animals do have a few rights too. I'm going to order this dog into protective custody until we can sort this thing out."

Now Jack let out with a string of cuss words and kicked the tire on his truck. "You people!" he burst out.

"Watch it, buddy!" said the sergeant.

Soon Sergeant Crane had collected the information he needed from an angry Jack and gave Alice instructions to take the dog to the vet. "Now, don't let me down," he told her as she opened the door to her car.

"I won't," she assured him, glancing nervously to where Jack was still standing nearby. "By the way," she said loud enough for Jack to hear. "I don't know if you knew it or not, but the woman you just arrested is a celebrity."

"A celebrity?" Sergeant Crane looked surprised, and it seemed that she had captured Jack's interest as well.

"Yes. Victoria Martin. She has a television show and knows all sorts of important people. Anyway, I'm sure there will be media coverage when they find out. Also, her lawyers will probably be coming soon."

He nodded. "Thanks for the heads up."

"A celebrity?" repeated Jack.

Alice nodded. "Yes. She probably would've paid dearly for that dog."

The man cussed angrily, then got into his truck and drove off.

"See you at the station?" said Sergeant Crane.

"I'll be there as soon as I drop Zipper off."

Chapter ❄ Twenty-Six

Alice felt slightly better to be entering the police station through the main entrance this time. "I'm here for Victoria Martin," she told the receptionist.

"*The* Victoria Martin?" asked the woman.

"That's right."

"Here?"

"Yes."

The woman nervously looked over her shoulder. "Is she doing one of her shows here or something?"

"Not exactly." Alice smiled. "She's been arrested."

The receptionist's eyes grew large. "Victoria Martin has been arrested?"

Alice nodded. "Sergeant Crane said that I could join her."

The receptionist shrugged. "Sure, fine. No one ever tells me anything around here."

"Thank you," said Alice as she went back to the office that she had visited just a few days before. She spied Victoria sitting in exactly the same chair that Alice had occupied on Wednesday. She was sitting slightly slumped over, still wearing her coat, with what looked like a cup of black coffee in her hands. It was her expression that stopped Alice. The poor woman looked as if she had lost her last friend, or someone had killed her dog.

"Victoria," said Alice.

Victoria sat a bit straighter. "Alice. I'm so glad you're here."

"Good news," said Alice as she pulled a chair up next to Victoria. "The sergeant let me take the dog. He's in protective custody."

Victoria brightened now. "Really?"

"Yes. I just dropped him at the vet."

"Oh, I'm so relieved."

"Have you called your attorney yet?"

"Yes, but I had to leave a message. He'll be checking his pager, I hope."

"Well, if this is anything like when I was in here, I'm sure they'll be releasing you soon."

"Do you think so?"

"Of course. I'm sure you don't have any prior convictions." Alice laughed.

"Don't be too sure."

Alice's eyes grew wider. "You do?"

"Just a couple of crazy things in college, during my drinking days, you know. Oh, and a minor scrap with a neighbor over a tree that he was trying to cut down—I could've sworn it was on my property. But those are in different states."

"Oh."

Unfortunately for Victoria, her previous record did,

indeed, show up. But Sergeant Crane was no fool. Instead of putting her in jail, he let her out on bail. Alice wrote a check for the required amount, since Victoria only had her American Express card with her. Despite Victoria's pleading, the Potterston Police Station did not take American Express.

"Don't leave home without it," she muttered as the two of them went out to find Alice's car. "Ha!"

"Hey, lady!" yelled a man from the other side of the street.

"Oh no," said Victoria. "It's that horrible man again. That crazy dog owner who got me into this mess."

"It's okay," said Alice. "We're right in front of the police station." Alice waved to an officer who was just coming out of the building. "He can't do anything to us here."

"I just want to talk to you," said the man as he jogged across the street.

"What do you want?" asked Victoria in the most imperious tone Alice had ever heard.

"Look, lady, I'm sorry about what happened at the track. You see, I've had a bad day—a bad month. My wife left me with three little kids a few weeks ago. I have a regular job, but dog racing helps to pay the bills, you know. And, believe it or not, Zipper was one of my favorite dogs, but he got disqualified at the track today."

"And what has this to do with me?" she demanded.

"Well, if you're still interested," he shrugged, "and you probably aren't, but I'd be willing to sell him."

"And what makes you think I want him now?" she demanded.

He shook his head now. "Fine. I figured as much." Then he started to walk away.

"Wait!" called Alice. "I might be interested."

He turned hopefully.

"I don't have a lot of money, but I—"

"Never mind." Victoria laid her hand on Alice's shoulder. "I want to buy the dog after all."

The man came back and looked at her. "Serious?"

She nodded solemnly. "Although things would've gone much simpler if we'd taken care of this *before* I was arrested."

"Yeah, it was pretty stupid on my part." He looked down at the ground. "Sorry 'bout that."

"All right," said Victoria in a firm voice. "I will purchase your dog from you, but only if you will march right back into the police station with me and tell them that you are not pressing charges."

"Fair enough."

Back they went to the police station. Fortunately, Sergeant Crane was not too busy and actually seemed rather pleased that they had reached an agreement. "It's refreshing to see citizens working out their problems outside of the court system," he told them as they finally finished the paperwork and returned the bail check to Alice.

Alice wrote Jack a generous check, for which Victoria would reimburse her later. After that, they stopped by the vet's.

"It's just a sprain," the vet assured them as Victoria paid the bill. Fortunately, the vet did take American Express. "But it's bad enough that you can be sure he'll never race again. Is that a problem?"

"Goodness, no," said Victoria. "I do not intend to race him." She smiled as she stroked the dog's smooth nose. "Although when he's better he'll probably enjoy giving Rob and Roy a run for their money. Rather, *my* money."

The vet looked slightly confused, although he nodded as if he understood. Alice suspected he thought he was dealing with a couple of batty old ladies.

Alice carried the still slightly sedated Zipper to her car and gently laid him in the backseat again. The dog licked her hand as if to say thanks as she put the blanket over him. "Now just rest there," she told him.

"Oh my," said Victoria as they were finally driving back toward Acorn Hill. "What a day."

Alice sighed. "I'll say."

"Something odd happened," said Victoria.

"Only *one* thing?"

"Well, one thing in particular. It happened when I was sitting in your backseat with Zipper. I experienced the most realistic flashback."

"What do you mean?"

Then Victoria launched into a story from her childhood. Her mother had died when she was nine years old and her father took her to her maternal grandparents to live. "It was only supposed to be a temporary thing," she said. "Just until my father got relocated and found work. After a while, I realized that he would never come back for me."

"I'm sorry," said Alice.

"My grandparents were good people, but they were rather cool and distant. They were quite a change from my parents, who had enjoyed lively music and friends and tended to laugh a lot. And although my grandparents weren't well off, they still seemed very formal and proper, at least to me. As a result, I suppose I felt like I was something of a burden to them so I tried to remain quiet and stay out of their way.

"Anyway, the event I just remembered happened on a Saturday. I was walking down an alley near my grandparents' home when I saw a boy from school. I knew that he was a bully, and I started to turn around and go the other way. Then I heard this pitiful yelping sound, and I could see that this boy had a puppy. I went a little closer and saw that he'd tied a rope around the puppy's neck, and he was swinging the poor little dog around and around as if he were a toy. Well, it was as if all the frustration and rage that I'd been keeping inside of me since my mother's death just burst to the surface, and like a wild girl I began screaming at him and beating on him with my fists until he dropped the poor dog and ran. Then I scooped up the limp puppy and, sobbing, I removed the rope and just held him to me and petted his coat. I still remember the silky feeling of his soft black fur. I started walking home, and by the time I got there, the puppy had come back to life."

"Oh my, what a brave and wonderful thing to have done," said Alice. "Did your grandparents let you keep him?"

"Well, I assumed they wouldn't allow me to have a pet. So I kept the puppy hidden in my room all weekend, sneaking him food when no one was looking. But by Sunday night, my grandfather discovered my secret. To my surprise, after I told him the story, my grandfather let me keep the pup. My grandmother, bless her heart, knit him a little blue sweater. That was when I began to see my grandparents in a whole new light."

"That's a great story," said Alice.

"I'd almost forgotten it," admitted Victoria. "Until I was sitting back there with Zipper. It's as if all those old protective feelings just came rushing back at me and I knew there was no way I was letting him go back with that Jack person."

"I don't think Jack was really so bad," said Alice. "As he said, he was having a bad week."

"But I'm sure he planned to dispose of his dog." Alice nodded sadly. "You're probably right."

Chapter ❄ Twenty-Seven

What took you two so long?" asked Jane when Alice came through the front door. "It's almost six o'clock."

Alice paused, holding the door open, until Victoria entered carrying the wounded dog.

"What on earth?" said Jane.

"This is Zipper," said Alice. "Victoria's new adoptee."

"Don't tell me you guys performed a rescue after we left." Jane reached over and patted the dog's head.

"Sort of," said Alice.

"Here," offered Jane, outstretching her arms. "You want me to help you with him?"

"Thanks," said Victoria as she handed the dog over to Jane. "Do you think it's okay if I keep him in my room? I'll gladly pay if anything gets damaged."

Jane glanced at Alice and she just shrugged.

"Sure," said Jane. "Why not."

"What's this?" asked Louise as she emerged from the dining room and spied Zipper. "Wendell just shot past me like a streak."

"This is Zipper," said Jane. "Victoria's new pet. Wendell will be okay when he gets used to him . . . I hope."

Jane and Victoria went upstairs with the dog, and Alice explained to Louise what had happened. "I'm sorry I didn't call," said Alice, "but everything happened so fast."

"Well, you better grab yourself a bite to eat. We ate early in order to get ready for the party. I shall take a tray up to Victoria."

"Thanks," said Alice. "It's been quite a day."

After a quick dinner, Alice went up to her room and took a shower, then sat down and put her feet up for a bit. She woke up to a knocking on her door.

"Alice?" called Jane.

"Come in," said Alice groggily, glancing at her clock to discover it was already seven.

"Are you okay?" asked Jane as she came into the room.

"Look at you!" Alice stood up and went over to examine Jane's costume. "You look just like Dorothy."

Jane laughed and held out her basket for Alice to see. "And Toto too."

"I must've fallen asleep. I'll get into my costume and be right down."

"Yes," said Jane with a bright smile. "You're missing the fun. Several people are already here and the costumes are wonderful."

It did not take Alice long to get into her scarecrow costume, humming "If I Only Had a Brain," as she dressed. She wished she could remember all the words to that tune, but maybe Jane could help her. Finally she went downstairs, where happy strains of music were pouring out of the parlor.

"Hi, Miss Howard," said Ashley as she came out of the dining room with a tray of canapés.

"How did you know it was me?" demanded Alice with some disappointment.

"Mrs. Smith, I mean Glinda the Good Witch, said you were the Scarecrow."

"And I know you are a Munchkin," said Alice.

Ashley did a mock curtsey. "Yes, and all of us Munchkins are going to do our song after more people get here." Then she lowered her voice. "You should see Mr. Tracy."

"What's he dressed like?"

"He's Willy Wonka," giggled Ashley.

"Who is Willy Wonka?" asked Alice.

"You know, Miss Howard, *Willy Wonka and the Chocolate Factory.*"

Alice nodded. It sounded vaguely familiar.

"He looks just like him too." Ashley grinned. "And his pockets are full of candy."

"Come in. Come in." Alice heard what sounded like Louise's voice, only at a slightly higher pitch, behind her. Surprised, Alice turned just in time to see her older, and normally reserved, sister wearing a long, blond curly wig and a sparkling blue gown. She gave a good imitation of Billie Burke's bubbling laugh as she waved a glittery wand at what appeared to be Lloyd and Ethel now entering the foyer.

"Aunt Ethel," said Louise. "Don't you look stunning."

"Why, thank you, Louise," laughed Ethel. "Or should I call you Glinda?"

"Hello," said Alice as she attempted a loose-jointed scarecrow-like bow.

"Alice?"

She did a little soft-shoe step and pointed her forefinger to her slightly cocked head. "Scarecrow to you," she said, then studied the pair. Lloyd wore tails, complete with white tie, top hat and cane. Ethel had on a golden satin gown and what appeared to be high-heeled tap shoes. "Who are you two supposed to be?" asked Alice. "You look very glamorous."

Ethel did a little tap step and held out her hand for Lloyd. "Your turn, Fred." Poor Lloyd was not quite as adept as his partner.

"Fred Astaire and Ginger Rogers?" ventured Louise.

"That's right," said Ethel as she gave her full skirt a swirl. "From *Swing Time.* Of course, I was probably still in diapers when that film came out."

"Of course," said Louise, winking at Alice.

"And look at you!" said Louise as someone came toward them from the dining room.

"Good evening, ladies and gentleman," said Harold as he tipped his stars-and-stripes hat.

"*Yankee Doodle Dandy*," said Alice, responding to the group's questioning look. Of course, she had had a heads-up on this one, or she would have been guessing with them.

"If you are in here, who is that playing piano?" asked Louise.

He grinned. "My backup, Patsy Ley."

"I didn't know Patsy could play so well," said Louise.

"Hidden talents," said Harold.

"What a great costume!" said Lloyd as he stepped up and took a better look at Harold's outfit. "Now, something like that would sure come in handy for my July Fourth speech."

"Perhaps we can work out a deal," offered Harold.

As if they were old friends, Harold and Lloyd continued to chat amicably as Alice went off to help in the kitchen.

"Actually I don't need help," said Jane. "Your

Munchkins seem to have things under control." She took Alice's arm. "I think we should join the others."

They picked up Louise and Cynthia on their way to the parlor, and waiting for a pause in the music, they made their entrance singing "We're Off to See the Wizard." Jane and Cynthia did most of the singing since Alice and Louise could not remember all of the words, but when they finished everyone in the room clapped loudly and demanded an encore.

Then, to the surprise of Alice and Jane, Louise and Cynthia did a wonderful rendition of "Over the Rainbow" that brought tears to Alice's eyes. Even though it was getting a bit stuffy beneath her scratchy burlap mask, she was thankful that it hid her tears.

It was not long before the party was in full swing and, despite the demands of a busy day, Alice found that she was having a wonderful time.

"Where's the Wicked Witch of the West?" asked Louise when it was getting close to eight. "You know, her costume arrived this afternoon. I put it in her room."

"Maybe a tornado dumped a house on her," said Alice as she waved at Wilhelm Wood. "Look at Wilhelm," she said to Louise, nodding toward the door where Wilhelm was wearing a tweed suit with vest and bow tie. He even had the perfect pipe to go with it.

"Who is he supposed to be? Sherlock Holmes?" asked Louise. "I don't recall any Sherlock Holmes musicals, do you?"

"No." Alice chuckled. "He and Sylvia coordinated

their outfits. She is coming as Eliza Doolittle from *My Fair Lady* and Wilhelm is supposed to be Henry Higgins, the stuffy fellow who tries to turn her into a lady."

"He looks so dignified in that old-fashioned suit."

"Oh, there's Sylvia now," said Alice, waving again.

"Oh my," said Louise. "Just look at her."

Heads turned when Sylvia entered the parlor and took Wilhelm's arm. No longer the shy and unassuming seamstress, Sylvia was bedecked in a beautiful lavender gown and matching hat.

"You look lovely," said Jane as she greeted her friend.

"Just like Eliza," said Sylvia with a smile.

Harold was back at the piano again, and Wilhelm was trying to get everyone's attention. "Miss Eliza Doolittle and I have a little number we'd like to perform." He cleared his throat and motioned to Sylvia, who was still talking with Alice and Jane.

Sylvia turned around and grinned at Wilhelm, and then sang out, "Just you wait 'enry 'iggins, just you wait." Everyone laughed, and before long she was joining him in singing "The Rain in Spain."

The evening went on with their friends and neighbors showing up in all sorts of getups and taking turns performing songs. Even elderly Clara Horn came dressed up like Miss Piggy. "In honor of my pet pig Daisy," she told everyone. "It was my granddaughter's idea."

Some of their guests sang quite expertly, while others were off-key and missed a few of the words, but it seemed that everyone was having a good time. The Munchkins were a huge hit when they sang. Craig Tracy gave all the girls candy and followed their performance with a number of his own, the "Oompa-Loompa" song.

"We should recruit him for the church choir," said Louise.

Jane nodded as she passed the platter of cheese puffs. "I'll mention it to him."

"And now for a little song and dance," announced Harold as Ethel and Lloyd took the floor. Lloyd only stepped on Ethel's feet a couple of times, and between the two of them, they were on key about half the time, but it was hard to beat their unbridled enthusiasm. They both bowed gracefully when their song, "A Fine Romance," was over. Naturally, the crowd clapped and cheered.

"Who knew that our mayor could sing and dance?" called out Fred Humbert.

"It hasn't been easy on my poor toes," said Ethel as she dramatically daubed her forehead with a handkerchief. "We only had a few evenings to practice, mind you."

"Yes," teased Lloyd, "and I thought Ethel would *never* learn the foxtrot."

"Oh pish posh," said Ethel.

Next Harold sang "Give My Regards to Broadway." As he finished, the crowd's attention turned toward the doorway as someone in black burst into the room making a wild cackling sort of laugh.

With her tall, pointed hat and her face painted green, Victoria made a spectacular entrance. She rushed over to where Jane was chatting with Craig Tracy and pointed a finger in her face. "I'll get you, Dorothy," she shrieked, "and your little dog too!"

"Oh dear," said Alice in her best dramatic voice, "it's the Wicked Witch of the West! Whatever shall we do?"

The room was quiet, as if the guests were expecting more.

"I'll take care of her," said Louise as she went over to where Jane was pretending to cower from Victoria. "I shall use my good magic on her," and Louise waved her wand over Victoria's pointed black hat. "From now on you shall be a good witch and only use your magic to help others."

"Oh," cried Victoria dramatically, "I think I'm melting." Then she pretended to be shrinking as she cried, "I'm melting, I'm melting."

The room erupted into a loud clapping and cheering, and Harold started playing another show tune.

"That was great," said Jane, patting Victoria on the back.

"My, yes," agreed Louise. "What an entrance. You must have taken acting lessons."

"I used to enjoy drama," said Victoria, pausing to rub her nose. "But I must admit that this green makeup is a bit irritating. Do you mind if I remove it?"

"No, not at all," said Alice, "and I'll take off this

mask. It makes it impossible for me to enjoy Jane's delectable treats."

Alice and Victoria retreated to the downstairs bathroom to alter their appearances. "How's Zipper?" asked Alice as she handed Victoria another tissue.

"He's sleeping soundly, poor guy." Victoria got the last of the green off and tossed the soiled tissue into the trash. "I think today wore him out."

"I took a nap too," admitted Alice. "If Jane hadn't awakened me, I'd probably still be snoozing."

"As would I," said Victoria as she adjusted her hat. "It was only the sounds of music and laughter that roused me."

"Sorry about that," said Alice as they went back out to join the party.

"Oh," said Victoria, "I was looking forward to this. It's really fun."

Alice smiled at her. "For the Wicked Witch of the West, you're being awfully congenial."

Victoria laughed. "I'm usually accused of being quite witchy, you know. I guess you and your sisters must have worn me down a bit this past week."

"I hear there is something in the water here in Acorn Hill," joked Alice. "It makes us all act a little nicer."

"Speaking of water . . ." Victoria leaned in and spoke in a quiet voice. "Before my entrance, I saw Wilhelm and he confessed something to me."

Alice's eyes grew wide. "About his tea?"

Victoria nodded.

"About his secret ingredient?"

220

Victoria laughed. "That tea did have a nice *smoky* quality to it."

"Poor Wilhelm," said Alice, "he felt perfectly horrible about the mistake."

"I don't know if it was such a mistake," said Victoria. "He's going to work on substituting other ingredients that would produce a similar flavor. He could be on to something." Victoria held her hands up as if she were about to cast a spell. "It might be perfectly magical." Then she flitted off to visit with the other guests.

The party lasted later than Alice and her sisters had expected. It was past midnight before the remaining guests, the lively Fred and Ginger, made their exit.

"Oh my," said Jane sinking into a chair and putting her ruby slippers on a footstool. "I am completely exhausted."

Louise removed her glittery crown and wig and sighed. "And I am ready to retire my crown for good."

"That was a great party," said Cynthia as she sank down onto the sofa. "You guys really know how to live."

Alice laughed and flopped down beside her.

"Did the Wicked Witch of the West already turn in?" asked Louise, glancing over her shoulder.

Cynthia nodded. "Yes, I warned her that I wanted to get an early start in the morning. I figured we could get a couple of hours in before church."

"And Harold called it a night too," said Alice. "I hope he didn't overtax himself."

"He looked as though he was having the time of his life," said Louise. "He was the hit of the party."

"I think Victoria's entrance was quite a hit too," said Alice. "Did you see the look on Aunt Ethel's face when she first came into the room?"

Cynthia nodded. "I thought poor Patsy Ley was going to faint."

"Talk about your drama queens," said Jane.

"She was a good sport," said Alice.

"Yes, she was," agreed Louise, "but I am not. My feet are aching from these pumps, and I am going to call it a night. I promise to rise early and help clean up in the morning."

"Yes," agreed Alice. "Let's *all* hit the hay."

Jane laughed. "Are you trying to make a joke, Scarecrow?"

Alice put on her Scarecrow voice. "Well, I would if I only had a brain."

"Oh, not again," said Jane groaning. "It's too late."

After turning off all the lights, the four of them went up the stairs softly humming "We're Off to See the Wizard."

Chapter ❄ Twenty-Eight

Alice awoke feeling strangely refreshed the next morning. She got up early and tiptoed downstairs and began picking up from last night's party. The house was quiet and still, and Alice was reminded of a time when it had nearly always been like this. When only she and Father lived there, the two of them would rattle around in this big old house. Would she return to those days if she could? Probably not, she thought as she threw another plastic punch cup into her trash bag. Living with her sisters and running the inn had become a wonderful way of life for her, and she did not want to give it up for anything.

"Alice." Jane had on her pale-gray sweats and her hair tied back in a messy ponytail. "How long have you been up?"

"Longer than you," teased Alice. "It looks like you just crawled out of bed."

Jane gave a stretch. "I did."

"There's coffee in the kitchen."

"You're a saint."

Alice just shook her head. "If only sainthood came so easily."

"It looks like you've just about got everything cleaned up.

"I figured I should, since I wasn't much use in getting things ready yesterday."

"Oh, there really wasn't that much," said Jane. "Especially after we'd gotten most of the food and stuff prepared ahead of time."

Alice picked up a few more things and then joined her sister in the kitchen.

"I put the teakettle on," said Jane as she sliced up a long loaf of French bread. "I think it's almost hot."

"Making French toast?" asked Alice when she noticed the eggs and cream nearby.

Jane nodded. "I thought I'd keep it simple."

"Sounds good to me."

"Hello," said Louise as she came into the kitchen. "It looks like the Brownies have already been here."

Alice laughed. "Do you remember when Mother used to say that after we'd try to surprise her by doing something?"

Louise nodded as she poured herself a cup of coffee. "And we would play right along."

All three sisters worked together to fix breakfast, and it was not long before the table was set and the others were joining them.

"How's the dog, Victoria?" asked Jane as she set a large bowl of homemade applesauce on the table.

"Zipper is doing fine," said Victoria as she poured herself a cup of coffee. "He ate the scraps that you gave me and even made an attempt to stand up on his own, but I think the leg still hurts too much. I carried him outside so that he could relieve himself."

"That's one lucky dog," said Harold as he set down the newspaper. Of course, everyone had heard the story by this time.

"I'll say," said Victoria. "If Alice and I had left just a couple minutes sooner, poor Zipper would probably be history now."

"There is a pet supply store in Potterston," said Alice. "It doesn't open until after noon on Sundays, but you could find some things for Zipper there."

"That's a good idea," said Victoria. "Perhaps Cynthia will let me take a little break and drive me over there."

Cynthia just shrugged. "Probably won't make a difference anyway."

"Is someone feeling discouraged?" asked Victoria in a slightly placating tone.

Cynthia held up her hands. "It just seems like we keep taking two steps forward and one step back. We only have three more days until our deadline."

Victoria frowned now. "Is that all?"

"That's all."

"Did you see the children's books that Vera dropped off?" asked Alice hopefully.

"I glanced at a few of them yesterday."

"Any inspirations?" asked Cynthia.

Victoria shook her head. "Not really."

Then Alice thought of something. "Of course, I don't really know much about publishing, but I do recall reading something once about the art of writing."

"Yes?" said Cynthia eagerly.

"Aren't writers supposed to write about what they know?"

Cynthia rolled her eyes. "Yes. That's usually the best route."

"Well, it just hit me that Victoria has a really wonderful animal story that actually happened to her as a little girl. Remember what you told me yesterday, Victoria?"

Now Victoria's eyes lit up. "Do you think?"

Alice nodded. "It was a lovely story."

"What?" demanded Cynthia. "What is it? Tell me, Victoria."

Victoria smiled. "Now, just hold your horses, Cynthia. I'm sure that the whole table isn't interested in my childhood memory."

"*Au contraire,*" said Jane as she sat back down at the table. "I'm interested."

"As am I," said Louise.

"I'd love to hear it," agreed Harold.

Now Victoria clasped her hands together as she looked around the table at her captive audience. "Well, then." Once again, Victoria related the story. This time she gave more details, and sensing that her listeners were interested, she added drama. Finally, she ended it by telling of her grandmother's knitting the little blue sweater.

Cynthia's face lit up. "I think we may have something here."

"Really?" Victoria seemed hopeful.

"Really." Cynthia pushed away her unfinished breakfast plate. "If you'll excuse me, I'd like to go start putting that in my computer. Just the bare bones, mind you. We'll flesh it out."

"Wonderful," said Victoria with a satisfied sigh.

"That's a great story," said Jane as she refilled Victoria's coffee cup.

"I thought so too," said Alice.

"I wonder," said Victoria. "Do you think there might be some way of tying Zipper's story into it?"

Jane frowned. "I'm no expert," she said, "but I think the story would have more impact if it was about rescuing one dog."

"Perhaps you could have a special section in the back of the book," suggested Alice, "making mention of how you rescued Zipper and that reminded you of when you were a little girl."

"That's an excellent idea," said Louise. "Maybe someone should be taking notes for Cynthia."

They sat around the dining room table, with Alice taking notes, as they did a little brainstorming for Victoria's book. Even Harold had a few ideas.

"Oh, this is really good," said Victoria as she stood up and reached for Alice's notes. "I can't wait to tell Cynthia our ideas."

Cynthia and Victoria became deeply involved in their efforts. Alice noticed that they were even later than the previous week in coming to church. Once again, they slipped into a rear pew, and to Alice's surprise, Victoria was treated less as a celebrity when the service was over.

"Looks like the locals are getting used to seeing her around," said Jane, nodding over to where only Patsy Ley was politely conversing with Victoria. Then Alice and Jane went over to ask how the book was progressing.

"It's amazing," said Cynthia. "Everything is just falling into place. I love Aunt Alice's idea about including something about the greyhound rescue in the back."

"Yes," said Victoria enthusiastically. "Cynthia has even suggested doing a photo shoot with me and my dogs."

"That would be a nice touch," said Jane.

"Speaking of dogs," said Alice, "would you like me to pick up some things for Zipper this afternoon? I thought it might be helpful since it seems like you and Cynthia have finally gotten on track."

"That'd be great," said Cynthia. "It really does feel like we're making progress. In fact, it was going so well that I was even tempted to skip church this morning. Then I remembered how you'd been praying that we'd come up with something, and I thought it would be ungrateful to bail out on God like that."

Alice laughed. "I don't think God would think you were bailing out on Him. Still, I'm glad you both came."

Then Victoria rattled off the things she thought that Zipper might need from the pet store.

"I'll head right over," said Alice as she buttoned up her coat.

"Need any company?" offered Jane.

They stopped at the inn to pick up Alice's car, but since it was not quite noon, they decided to drop by the Coffee Shop. As they were about to enter, Alice heard someone calling her name. She turned to see Carlene Moss hurrying down the street toward them.

"Have you got a minute, Alice?" she called out breathlessly.

"Of course."

"I thought you might enjoy hearing the latest news," Carlene said.

"What's that?"

"Well, remember there were a number of high school kids at your demonstration yesterday?"

"Yes, but it wasn't really *my* demonstration," said Alice.

Carlene smiled. "Yes, I know, but anyway it seems that some of the protesters from yesterday's march are going to organize a greyhound adoption group. I had a message on my voice mail this morning asking if I would cover the story in the *Acorn Nutshell* this week. Apparently there were two teenage boys who helped you and Victoria with that greyhound yesterday, and they were so impressed with your saving that dog that they want to do more of the same."

"That's fantastic!" Alice clapped her hands with enthusiasm.

Carlene nodded. "Not only that, but a dog owner called. He wanted to go on record that there were many caring dog owners and that they were all in favor of regulations to protect the dogs. Anyway, I'd like to get some quotes from you and from Victoria, and maybe a photo of the dog. Do you think you could call me later today or tomorrow?"

"Of course. You know that I'd be happy to do anything to help this cause."

Carlene patted Alice on the back. "You've already done a lot, Alice. You got the ball rolling and that's a lot more than anyone else was doing."

"How nice that the local teens want to join the cause," said Jane. "I'll bet they can really generate enthusiasm."

"Thanks for telling us," said Alice. "I'll pass the information along to Victoria."

"Be in touch," said Carlene as she headed across the street.

"Isn't that wonderful," said Alice as she pushed open the door to the Coffee Shop.

"It's great." Jane sniffed the air. "*Hmmm*. I haven't had a slice of blackberry pie in ages."

Alice laughed. "Do you really think we should? After all, we had French toast for breakfast."

"That was breakfast," said Jane with a grin. "It's lunchtime now."

"So it is," said Alice as they sat down at the counter.

"Hey, you two," said Hope. "That was quite a party last night."

"I liked your Mary Poppins outfit," said Alice. "Very clever."

"And your rendition of 'A Spoonful of Sugar' wasn't bad either," added Jane.

"I think you should have a party like that at least once a year," said Hope as she set two water glasses in front of them.

"We'd have to talk Harold into coming back," said Jane.

"I overheard him telling Viola Reed that he was considering buying a place and moving here permanently," Hope told them.

"Wouldn't that be nice," said Alice.

"We're both having pie," said Jane with a slightly guilty expression.

"Blackberry?" asked Hope.

Alice and Jane both nodded.

"À la mode?"

They exchanged glances, and then nodded again.

"Some things never change," said Hope with a grin.

Chapter ❄ Twenty-Nine

Victoria's book was finished by Monday afternoon. In celebration, Jane fixed a special dinner.

"It's completely edited and on its way," announced Cynthia at dinner. "My boss will have it on his desk tomorrow."

"Signed, sealed and delivered," said Victoria.

"Congratulations to you both," said Harold, holding up his water glass in a toast. "Here's to its becoming a classic."

Everyone else raised her glass with him.

"And to touching the hearts of children," added Alice.

"And to selling a million copies," said Jane.

As they were sitting around the table after dinner, Harold also announced that he, like Cynthia and Victoria, would be checking out the next day.

"It's been a delightful time," he told them, "but I fear I've overstayed my welcome."

Naturally, they all protested that this was not true.

"Oh, I'm sure Louise will be happy to have her piano all to herself." He winked at her.

Louise shook her head. "The truth is I have begun to develop an appreciation for music other than the classics. Just seeing what a good time everyone had on Saturday night reminded me that sometimes we need a change of pace."

"Here, here," said Jane.

"We've heard a rumor," Alice said to Harold. "Is it true that you're thinking of moving to Acorn Hill?"

He laughed. "Well, I don't know. I'll have to go home and see how I like it there. You ladies have all given me hope that there is life beyond what I've been living. I'll see how it goes in Philadelphia, and if I don't like it there, well, you just never know. One thing you can count on." He smiled at all of them. "I do plan to come back to visit."

"Oh good," said Jane. "Our friends are already making plans for next year's show-tunes party. Sylvia said that she's had several people in her shop talking about what kinds of costumes they'd like her to help them with for next year."

"That reminds me," said Harold. "I wanted to leave my costume for your mayor. He thought perhaps he could use it for the Fourth of July."

Jane laughed. "I can just see Lloyd wearing something like that."

"Maybe Aunt Ethel will want to have one made to match," said Alice.

"Speaking of Lloyd and Aunt Ethel," said Louise,

"have you heard the latest?"

"Oh dear," said Alice. "What's wrong now?"

"Nothing's wrong," said Louise. "After Saturday's party, Aunt Ethel talked Lloyd into giving up bowling."

"Really?" Jane looked disappointed. "I thought it was sort of cool that he'd turned into a bowler."

"Well, apparently, he has not been doing too well at it," continued Louise, "and Aunt Ethel has convinced him that the two of them should take tap-dancing lessons together."

"Tap-dancing lessons," repeated Victoria. "How interesting."

"Where will they do that?" asked Alice.

"I believe that the Potterston senior center offers a class."

"Fred and Ginger," said Jane. "Now if Aunt Ethel could only learn how to carry a tune."

"*Whoa,* is that ever the pot calling the kettle black, Aunt Jane," said Cynthia.

They all laughed as Alice and Jane began to clear away the dishes.

Chapter ❄ Thirty

It is nice and quiet around here," said Alice as she and her three sisters sat in the sunroom and watched the snowflakes falling from the pewter-colored sky. It was Alice's first day off since their three guests had left.

Jane took a sip of cocoa and sighed. "Yes, it is rather nice, after all."

"Oh?" Louise's brow lifted slightly. "Did I hear my youngest sister admitting that she sometimes enjoys a little peace and quiet?"

Jane smiled. "I suppose so."

"It was sort of fun having all that activity too," said Alice. Wendell purred as she ran her hand down his thick winter coat. "Still, I do enjoy a little bit of winter quiet."

Louise sighed. "Especially on days like this."

"It looks like there's almost two inches of snow now," said Jane as she refilled their cocoa cups.

"And two more expected before nightfall," said Alice.

"Cynthia called this morning," said Louise. "She said that the publisher loves Victoria's book."

"That's wonderful," said Alice. "Did she say how their trip home went? Was the dog okay?"

"Sounded like it went fine," said Louise.

"He seemed like a sweet dog," said Jane, "but I'll bet he'll be a handful once he starts feeling better."

"Well, Victoria has lots of space for dogs who like to run," said Alice. "Not only that, but she told me she had a professional trainer work with her other dogs and she plans to get him for Zipper as well."

"Imagine," said Jane. "Having that much money."

"Money doesn't buy happiness, Jane," said Louise.

"If I were in Victoria's shoes," said Jane, "I'm sure that I would be happy as a clam."

"Don't be so sure," said Alice. "Victoria's life hasn't been nearly as charmed as she lets people believe."

"What?" said Jane with curiosity. "Did she tell you something?"

Alice just shook her head. "I'm only saying that things aren't always what they seem. It's possible that someone like Victoria would like to trade places with someone like you, Jane."

Jane waved her hand. "Oh yeah, sure."

"Are you saying that you do not have a good life?" asked Louise.

"No, not at all," said Jane as she took another piece of banana nut bread from the plate and pulled up the red plaid throw more snugly around her legs. "I love my life."

Alice smiled and leaned back in her chair contently. "So do I."

Louise nodded. "It is nice, isn't it?"

They sat quietly for a while, just soaking in the silence and the pristine white beauty of the snow blanketing all around the sunroom. Alice watched as the bare branches of the maple tree became dusted with a coating of white.

"Oh my goodness," said Louise reaching into her skirt pocket. "I almost forgot, Jane. There was a card for you in the mail today. I did not mean to snoop, but it looks as if it is from Victoria."

"You're kidding," said Jane as she eagerly reached for the envelope. "Victoria actually wrote something to me?" She examined the exterior of the pale green envelope with suspicion. "Maybe it's a recipe for the *proper* way to prepare a crown roast."

Louise and Alice waited as she carefully tore open the envelope and extracted a pretty note card with a pressed flower on the front.

"What does it say?" Louise demanded finally.

"Yes," said Alice as she tried to read Jane's expression, "don't keep us in suspense."

"Shall I read it aloud?"

"Please," urged Alice.

"Okay." Jane looked as if she was suppressing a smile.

Dear Jane,

I wanted to take a moment from my busy schedule to thank you for being such an exemplary hostess and chef during my stay at your family's inn. Although I may not have mentioned it, I found your cooking to be some of the finest I have had the pleasure to enjoy. You see, I have learned over the years to be sparing in my compliments in the areas of cooking and homemaking because I am so often accosted by people who hope to be invited to make an appearance on my show. But I do not fear that will be the case with you.

Jane stopped reading and giggled.

"*And?*" queried Louise. "Is that all?"

"Not quite."

Louise and Alice both watched their younger sister, waiting for her to continue.

Jane continued in a Victorialike voice.

And because I feel so comfortable with you and your sisters and in your lovely inn, I am certain that I shall be making it one of my regular get-away spots in the future.

Louise's eyebrow arched. "Seriously?"

"That's what it says," said Jane. "And it is signed, 'Fondly, Victoria.'"

"Oh my," said Alice, "how do you feel about her visiting again?"

Jane replaced the note card in its envelope. "Well, I should have known that God wasn't finished with me yet."

"Oh, *Jane*," said Louise.

Alice laughed. "I think we can all be very thankful that God is never finished with any of us."

"More cocoa?" offered Jane with a small smile.

"Thanks," said Alice.

Louise sighed. "I just love the quiet wonders of a snowy, winter day."

Tomato Bisque
SERVES SIX

3 tablespoons butter

1 medium onion, coarsely chopped

2 tablespoons all-purpose flour

2 cups water

4 pounds tomatoes, peeled, seeded and cut into pieces

2 tablespoons light brown sugar

6 whole cloves

1 teaspoon salt

Freshly ground black pepper

I cup light cream or whipping cream

Over medium heat, melt the butter in a large saucepan. Add the onion and stir until onion is tender. Sprinkle in flour and continue stirring until mixture foams. Stir in water and bring to a boil. Measure out ¾ cup of the tomato pieces and set aside for later. Add the remaining tomato pieces to the boiling mixture. Stir in the brown sugar and cloves. Reduce the heat and simmer, uncovered, for thirty minutes.

Transfer to a sieve and pass the mixture through. Return to the saucepan and stir in the remaining ¾ cup of tomato pieces. Blend in the salt, pepper and cream. Place over medium heat and warm gently, but do not boil. Serve immediately.

Center Point Publishing
600 Brooks Road • PO Box 1
Thorndike ME 04986-0001 USA

(207) 568-3717

US & Canada:
1 800 929-9108
www.centerpointlargeprint.com